Starting

from Scratch

Also by Jazz Taylor

Meow or Never

Starting from Scratch

Jazz Taylor

SCHOLASTIC INC.

Copyright © 2023 by Jazz Taylor

All rights reserved. Published by Scholastic Inc., *Publishers since 1920*. SCHOLASTIC and associated logos are trademarks and/or registered trademarks of Scholastic Inc.

The publisher does not have any control over and does not assume any responsibility for author or third-party websites or their content.

No part of this publication may be reproduced, stored in a retrieval system, or transmitted in any form or by any means, electronic, mechanical, photocopying, recording, or otherwise, without written permission of the publisher. For information regarding permission, write to Scholastic Inc., Attention: Permissions Department, 557 Broadway, New York, NY 10012.

This book is a work of fiction. Names, characters, places, and incidents are either the product of the author's imagination or are used fictitiously, and any resemblance to actual persons, living or dead, business establishments, events, or locales is entirely coincidental.

ISBN 978-1-338-80329-7

10 9 8 7 6 5 4 3 2 1   23 24 25 26 27

Printed the U.S.A.   40
First printing 2023

Book design by Omou Barry

To Grandma, always.
And to the girls rediscovering themselves—
I hope you choose to be whoever
makes you happy.

Chapter 1

There's a best way to do everything.

If I get up at exactly 6:32 a.m., I won't ever be late for school. If I put my hairbrush in the same place every morning, I'll never lose it. If I write Mom's appointments on her calendar as soon as she tells me about them, I won't ever forget to remind her. Everything has its place, its time, its order.

But Mom doesn't understand that. Which is why I'm about to be late for Sunshine Club, something that's been part of the schedule for a whole year and a half.

"Mom," I say, trying not to fidget. "Please, I can't miss

Sunshine Club today. It's the last one before we go back to school! Lula will miss me." Lula is my friend who lives at Elk Ridges nursing home. We visit her every week, and we always play checkers and gossip about the other residents. I really love talking with her, even though she never lets me win our game.

"You can," Mom says, smiling at me. She's taking cookies out of the oven, so our kitchen is warm and the air hangs heavy with sugar. "And you will! Lula will understand. This is important."

"But I always go to Sunshine Club on Thursdays. At four." Every Thursday, for over a year. Every Monday too. But Mom always forgets, and I have to remind her at least once a month. And now, clearly.

"I know, Janie," Mom says, still smiling. "However, your new sister doesn't move in every Thursday!"

That's true, I guess. But Mom didn't tell me it meant missing Sunshine Club for her. It's not fair. I barely even know her! And I have a schedule. Bad things happen when we get off our schedule.

I glance at my watch. If we don't leave in five minutes, I'll be late. Mom isn't even dressed. She's still wearing pajama pants. "Can't we just take Makayla with us?"

Mom looks up at the ceiling, and my heart stutters with hope. "Actually, Janie, that is *such* a good idea. She won't have friends here yet. I'm really proud of you."

I smile up at her. "Thanks, Mom. So we can go?"

"Sure! Next time." Mom winks at me. "Today, you're going to welcome Keisha and Makayla into our home."

I close my eyes, defeated. It's over. We'll never make it now. I sigh and slink into the living room to wait for Keisha to bring Makayla over from picking things up at her dad's house.

Getting a new sister was not part of my schedule. *Any* schedule. In May, Mom brought a new "friend" to the school's end-of-the-year party. And I thought that was fine—Mom makes a ton of new friends all the time because of her art studio. But then that "friend" hung out with us all summer. And then she started saying, "Oh, Janie, you can call me Keisha and not Ms. Jones." And then when school started again, this "friend" was at our house all the time and eating dinner with us. And

3

before I knew it, I was helping Mom's "friend" pick out a wedding ring.

And, I mean, it's fine. Keisha is fine. I like her okay, and she makes Mom really happy. That's what I like the most about her. But Keisha also has a daughter, and she's twelve just like me. So now I have a stepsister, one who I don't know at all because she went to a different middle school before now, and a stepmother who I know a little better but not that much.

Again, this is fine. I've already cried a little and panicked a little, and now I'm calm. I've decided that doubling our family size isn't so bad. And Dani, my best friend, reminded me that at least I don't have to move houses and schools like Makayla. It'll be fine. Maybe even fun! Maybe Makayla likes baking and dogs. Maybe it'll be easy to add two more people to the schedule. Though it is a little ominous that I'm *already* having to change my schedule and Makayla isn't even here yet . . .

I slump onto the couch and pull out my phone to text Dani a thumbs-down. Dani immediately responds with *tragedy*. I wait for more, but she just sends me a downhearted emoji and the orange heart. She's trying to find which one she likes the best (very important for her "image," she says), so I've gotten every color this week. I start to tell her to please say hi to Lula for me and don't forget to remind everyone to make the new flyers for Sunshine Club, but my thumbs freeze when I hear the crunch of gravel outside.

I scramble to my feet. "Mom, they're here!"

"Okay," Mom calls from the kitchen, but she doesn't come into the living room. I straighten my shirt, a little nervous. I've only seen Makayla a handful of times, once at the art gallery, a few parties in the summer, and at the wedding two months ago. We didn't talk much at any of them. And now she's going to live with us. Her room is all set up and everything. I've known about this move since the wedding, but it still doesn't feel real. Even now, as footsteps approach the house.

The door opens. I see Keisha first. She's shorter than Mom, has really pretty dark skin, and she always wears her firefighter boots. Like, all the time, even when she's not at work. Dani would call this "effective branding," but I think it's a little weird.

Don't her feet get tired? Keisha usually wears a big smile, but she brightens even more when she sees me. "Hey, Janie! Were you waiting for us?"

"Yes," I say. I want to say more, but I can't think of anything that sounds right.

Keisha steps into the house, and then I see Makayla. She's wearing a light green shirt and jeans, and her hair is in thick braids. Her skin tone is a little lighter than Keisha's, almost the same as mine. She has two suitcases, even though she only goes to her dad's house every other weekend. She must have a lot of clothes, which I can respect. Makayla meets my eyes, but then quickly looks down at her purple tennis shoes.

"Hi," I offer. She doesn't say anything, so now I'm fidgeting. Should I ask about her trip? But then that sounds like I'm being nosy. And, I mean, I *am* curious about this mysterious Dad I've never seen, but I feel like I shouldn't ask that right away. I'll just wait for her to talk.

Makayla looks up as Keisha pats her back and goes to the kitchen, leaving us alone. Makayla still hasn't come inside . . .

and the door is wide open. We're letting the heat out, as Lula would say.

"Umm, hi," Makayla finally says. She pushes up her glasses and readjusts her grip on the second suitcase. "I guess I, uh, live here now."

I smile at her. She's kinda awkward, but not bad awkward. "Yeah, you do. Do you want to come in?"

Makayla looks shocked, like she's just realized she's still standing outside. "Oh, yeah, sorry." She steps into the living room, dragging her suitcases behind her, and closes the door. Should I offer to take her stuff up to her room? I don't know . . . I've never had a sister before. It's just been me and Mom for as long as I can remember.

"Umm, do you want some cookies? Mom made some."

"Oh, that's okay." Makayla shifts from foot to foot. "I ate at Dad's."

I want to ask about this Dad *so bad*! But it would be rude, I know. I pick something else to say. "That's okay, maybe later? I can actually make us some. I'm pretty good at baking."

"Oh, cool." Makayla gives me a tentative smile. "I'm not really into cooking that much. But it's cool you are."

Oh, she doesn't like baking . . . I push away the twinge of disappointment. Maybe we can find something else in common.

"That's fine! It's probably better if—"

I'm cut off by a small noise from Makayla's second suitcase. It's like . . . a baby? A doll or something?

"Oh, sorry, she's probably cranky." Makayla bends down and unzips the suitcase. Which I'm now realizing . . . is not a suitcase. It's a cloth pet carrier.

I watch in horror as two orange ears poke out of the carrier. And then a small head, and a large, round body. It's a cat. A CAT.

I hate cats!!

"This is Pumpkin," Makayla says happily.

Pumpkin. A good name for it, considering it's orange and very round. But why is it *here*?

"Oh, that's, umm . . ." I back away as Pumpkin sniffs my tennis shoes. "Is it just visiting? For the weekend?"

Makayla frowns. "No, she doesn't really like Dad, and she gets sad when I'm gone. So we brought her here."

I clear my throat, but the lump lodged in it doesn't go away. "But, like, not permanently, right?"

"Umm . . ." Makayla's smile disappears. She wrings her hands anxiously. "Do you not like cats?"

I don't answer her because Mom and Keisha finally come into the living room. Mom's holding a tray of cookies, but before she can speak, I point to Pumpkin, who is now sniffing the bottom of the couch. "Mom, Makayla brought her cat."

"Oh, yeah!" Mom says, smiling. "I forgot to tell you, Janie, my bad."

My bad, she says. I can't believe this. I can't believe Mom would agree to this! She knows I hate cats! Ever since Grandpa's cat scratched me, I've hated them. They're so hissy and bitey and not cute like dogs are!

"You're making a scary face, Janie," Keisha teases.

"I thought you'd be more excited," Mom says, frowning at me. "You're always asking for a pet. And now we have one!"

A dog. I've been asking for a *dog* for years, not a pet. Not a cat! And this one is glaring at me, settling onto our couch like it lives here.

Well. I guess it does.

"Excuse me," I say weakly. "I need to go upstairs."

"Are you feeling okay?" Keisha asks. She's frowning now too.

"I'm fine," I say, halfway to the stairs. "Oh, uh, Makayla, see you later."

I don't wait for anyone to call me back. I run to my room, close the door, and collapse face-first onto my bed.

This is a lot to handle. Makayla doesn't like baking *or* dogs. Well, maybe she likes dogs, but if she has a cat, I'm sure she prefers them. And the cat! I can't believe I have to live with something that might scratch me at any moment. I can't believe Mom forgot I didn't like cats. Or maybe she didn't care.

I close my eyes and sigh into my pillow. This new family thing is going to be a lot harder than I thought.

Chapter 2

My alarm goes off at exactly 6:32 a.m., and I sit straight up in bed. Time to get ready for school.

I jump out from under my covers and go to my closet. I already picked out my clothes last night, so all I have to do is brush my teeth and do my hair. Efficiency is the key to any routine! And repetition. I don't even really need my alarm in the morning now. My body just knows when it's time for school. That does make sleeping in on weekends hard though.

I pull on my favorite, Muppets-themed socks, feeling pretty good. It's been a few days since Makayla moved in, and it's not so bad. I've been trying to be friends with Makayla, but I can't quite figure her out. She's really shy, and she stays in her room most of the time. Which is okay! She'll be with us for a long time, probably, so I don't want to bother her when she's only been here for a few days. I just make sure to listen when she wants to talk about cats. Even though I don't like them.

Speaking of cats: The situation is not *ideal*, but I'm surviving. Things looked bleak after Pumpkin's appearance, but Makayla keeps Pumpkin in her room, so I can just ignore the cat. Makayla loves it—her, I mean—very much, so I don't have any chance of Pumpkin moving back to the mysterious Dad's. Also, apparently, it's rare for orange cats to be girls so Makayla is super proud of her. I learned this in a very enlightening conversation with Makayla about all things cat. I now know what a tabby is, so I feel a little smarter.

I lace up my tennis shoes and straighten my shirt. Everything will work out. I can avoid Pumpkin, I can be friends with Makayla, I can talk to Keisha like normal. I can do this. I check my watch—6:38. Right on time! I go to the bathroom, ready to brush my teeth and my hair—and I stop.

Makayla's in here.

"Hi, Janie," she mumbles, rubbing her eyes. She's still in her pajamas. She has her toothbrush in one hand and she yawns. "I didn't sleep at all last night. I guess I'm kinda nervous about school."

We only have one sink, one mirror. I blink at her, dread building in my belly, my heart thudding against my ribs. I didn't account for this in the schedule.

"Oh, do you want to go first?" Makayla asks. She steps backward, but I shake my head.

"No, it's, umm, it's okay. I'll just—I'll just get my backpack together."

I leave the bathroom and go back to my room, but I just stand there for a minute. I've had the same school routine since I was in the third grade. This is the first time I've had to change it in years.

It's fine. I'm fine. I'll adjust! That's what I tell myself, but I'm confused. I don't know what to do first. I need to gather my pencils and notebooks, but maybe I should run downstairs and grab a Pop-Tart first? No, wait, I haven't brushed my teeth yet—

"Janie, I'm done!" Makayla calls, making me jump. I'm still holding all my school books and not moving. I check my watch—six minutes behind. I'll have to hurry, but I can do it. I have to. We have to be on time, especially for the first day of the new semester!

I run into the bathroom to brush my teeth as fast as I possibly can. I wash my face, check my teeth again, and brush my hair with lightning speed. Done! I stuff my planner and books into my backpack and run downstairs, just ten minutes later than usual.

"Did you sleep late?" Mom asks me, yawning and pouring coffee into a mug with an elephant decal on the front. Keisha and Makayla are in the kitchen too, but they're talking to each other. Makayla looks a little scared . . . she did say she was nervous.

"No," I tell Mom and search the pantry for the strawberry

Pop-Tarts. "I'll have to wake up earlier to stay on schedule. Totally my fault."

Mom smiles and yawns again. "You and that schedule . . ."

I find the Pop-Tarts and check my watch again. Twenty minutes left for breakfast. Plenty of time. "Did you remember to take your medicine?"

"Yep," Mom says.

"Did you *really* remember, or are you just saying that?"

Mom laughs and gives me a hug. I smile too, but I'm not done. She didn't answer my question.

"I saw her take them," Keisha says, startling me. She grins, one hand on Makayla's shoulder. "I'll keep an eye on her, don't worry."

"Oh, okay . . ." I fidget with the wrapping of my Pop-Tart, a strange discomfort in my chest. I've always been the one to remind Mom about her meds.

"Anyway, ready to go, girls?" Keisha asks.

I shake my head, confused. Mom always drives me to school. And it's too early! We still have eighteen minutes! "But Mom is driving me—us—right?"

"Nope," Mom says. "Keisha's gonna take you both, since it's on her way to work."

My chest tightens with more discomfort. Another setback?! I didn't prepare for any of this! "But why so early? Normally I leave at seven fifteen."

"It's the first day!" Keisha says. "Can't be late!"

"But we won't be late if we leave at seven fifteen—"

"Go on, Janie," Mom interrupts me, smiling. She nudges me gently toward the door. "Have a good day!"

No, this is all wrong . . . my stomach twists into anxious knots. We have to stay on schedule. We have to, or else. But Keisha already has the car keys and Makayla is heading to the front door, and getting left behind is worse than being early. I groan a little, but shoulder my backpack and decide I can eat in the car. School twenty minutes earlier it is.

I remind Mom of her work meeting and give her a hug, and then run after Keisha and Makayla. We both sit in the back seat (though Mom always used to let me sit up front with her). Keisha cranks up the car and glances back at us.

"Ready for your first day of the semester, girls?"

I nod, but Makayla looks like she's going to be sick.

"It's not bad," I tell Makayla as Keisha pulls out of our driveway. Mom waves at us from the porch, and I wave back.

"Yeah," she says, her voice strained. She twists her backpack straps between her fingers.

Wow, she's *really* nervous. Poor Makayla. I was nervous my first day of middle school too. And I was already friends with Dani then. I try to think of something to say, but it's probably better to eat my Pop-Tart in silence. She might be embarrassed, and me pointing out how nervous she is might make things worse.

Predictably, we arrive at school way before everyone else. Normally, I'd meet Dani, Piper, and Kyle outside Piper's homeroom and we'd talk, but now I have to wait twenty-two whole minutes with nothing to do. I hate having nothing to do. I'll have to convince Keisha to get on the regular schedule tomorrow.

Makayla and I hop out of the car while Keisha waves at us. "Have a good day! Love you!"

"Bye," Makayla says, and her voice sounds like she'll never see Keisha again.

We wave and Keisha speeds away. Makayla shifts from foot to foot, looking at the ground. "Umm, I guess I'll see you around. I'll go find, uh . . ." Makayla pulls a piece of paper from her pocket. "Mrs. Jenkins's class?"

Oh man, this is kinda sad. She's so nervous she looks like she'll pass out. I have to do something. "Hey, we have extra time before school starts. Let me see your schedule."

She gives me a (very sweaty) piece of paper. I scan it quickly—we have three classes together. This won't be bad at all. "Okay, you have math, science, and history with me. And you have English and art with my friend Piper. This'll be great, don't worry. Want me to show you around?"

Makayla nods, gratitude all over her face. "Yeah. Thank you, Janie."

I try to put on an encouraging expression. "No problem. Come on, let's start the tour."

Makayla and I walk around the school twice. I show her the

classrooms, and where to sit at lunch, and the best shady spot in the courtyard to sit on our breaks. By the time we get to her last class, art, she seems a lot calmer.

"What do you think?" I ask, handing her paper back.

"I feel a lot better," she says. She gives me a tentative smile. "Thanks, Janie."

I smile back. A stepsister wasn't part of the schedule, but so far, it's not bad at all. After Makayla finds some friends, she'll be fine! Speaking of . . . "Have you picked your club yet?"

She shakes her head. "No, I think I'll just go home after school."

"No way! Here, I'll show you something." I check my watch, but we still have seven minutes before homeroom. I lead Makayla to the building where all the clubs meet, and into the third room on the right.

"This is Sunshine Club! It's a volunteer club, and we do all kinds of things. We meet every Monday and Thursday after school for an hour and a half." I try not to sound too excited, but I'm about to burst with pride. Sunshine Club is so important to me. Dani and I joined last year when we were sixth graders, when there were only three people (me and Dani included). And now there are ten of us! We spent so much time recruiting and handing out posters and deciding what types of activities to do . . . it's amazing. It's the first place I could really relax.

Makayla looks around the room, and she actually seems . . . happy?! "Wow, I love it! What kind of volunteering?"

"Mondays are a free-for-all. A lot of the time we use it for planning, then sometimes we give out cookies to strangers, or we clean Eagle Park, or we go to the food bank, all kinds of stuff. But every Thursday we go to Elk Ridges, which is a nursing home." I pause, remembering Pumpkin. "But you might not like that one, because our advisor brings her dog too. She's a therapy dog. Her name is Buttons." And she's *so cute* with her snow-white fur, tiny black nose, and huge, bright eyes. She's exactly the kind of dog I wanted. But I guess I'm stuck with Pumpkin the too-fat cat for a while.

"Oh no, that's okay! I like dogs too."

I can't hold in a gasp. I just assumed she wouldn't like them . . . ! Maybe Makayla and I can be friends after all.

"So . . . will you join?" Maybe I'm sounding too eager. I clear my throat. "I mean, there's no pressure. There are a bunch of other clubs."

Makayla gives me a big smile. "I'd love to join! Actually, I was in a club like this last year, but it was called Kindness Club. And I really loved it, but I had to quit because . . ."

Suddenly, Makayla stops talking and her face falls. A dark, troubled expression replaces her smile. It's like someone flipped a light switch.

I frown too. I wonder what happened at her other club . . . ? There's so much I want to ask Makayla about—her dad, how she tolerates cats, and now this. But Lula says I should always mind my own business. I don't want to be rude, and really, we just met. She'll tell me if she wants to.

"Well, you'll love Sunshine Club. Promise."

She smiles again, but it's a little sad this time. "Yeah. Thanks for asking me to join."

The warning bell rings and Makayla jumps. I smile at her encouragingly. "Come on, let's get to homeroom. Hopefully the day goes by quickly, because we have a club meeting to look forward to!"

Makayla nods, and we leave Sunshine Club to go back to the main building. She walks close to me, too close to be honest, but I don't mind. Maybe having a sister won't be so bad after all.

Chapter 3

As soon as the bell rings to signal the end of my last class, I rush to Sunshine Club. I need to get there before Makayla so I can introduce her to everyone. After spending the day with her, I think she'll need some help making friends. When our math teacher asked Makayla to introduce herself, she nearly fainted.

I round the corner and can't help but smile. Dani's leaned against the wall, arms crossed, her snapback tilted to one side. She's wearing blue leggings with tiny white walruses on them and a new jacket (is that leather? Really?). Admittedly, today she looks pretty cool. Dani is obsessed with being cool, but not the usual route of being popular. She wants to find "peak coolness," whatever that means. She babbles about brands and stuff, and I don't really get it, but my job is to tell her when she's being "true cool" versus "fake cool." Today, standing against the wall with a faraway expression in her light brown eyes, with her new snap-back and walrus leggings, she's pretty cool. I move closer to tell her that, but as soon as she sees me, she leaps away from the wall and a huge grin lights up her face. I smile back. Maybe I'm biased, but being excited to see your best friend is pretty cool to me.

"JV!" We slap our palms together, do a fist bump, then cross our pointer fingers together in an X. I'm not into secret hand-shakes, but Dani says they're "coming back in style," so here we are. "How's the new sister deal going?"

"Good."

Dani wrinkles her nose. She's got cute freckles a few shades darker than her brown skin, so it's kind of adorable. "That sounds like a 'not-so-good' in disguise."

"She's fine, I swear." And she is. It's just everything she

brought with her that's *not* fine . . . my mind goes to Pumpkin uneasily. I'll die if she's in my room when I get home.

"Hmm, sounds like a classic case of Janie denial." Dani puts her hand to her chin, like she's deep in thought. "You should be open to new experiences, but be honest with yourself if it get be too much." I start to answer, but she suddenly gasps. "Oh my god, JV, I sounded so cool just now."

"It's less cool when you say that."

We laugh and some of the stress eases from my shoulders. Dani and I have been friends for forever, since before I can really remember, and she always makes me relax. She's the only one I don't mind being myself with.

Dani elbows me playfully. "What do you want to do tomorrow?"

Every Tuesday and Friday after school, I hang out with Dani. She thinks it's dumb I have certain days and times to hang out, but I like it. "You pick. No more eating contests though—I threw up last time."

"Weak!" Dani laughs and I do too. "Oh, what if we invited your sister along?"

I gasp. I forgot about Makayla! She'll be here any minute! "Hold on for a second. Are Piper and Kyle in the clubroom already?" Dani nods, frowning, and I grab her hand. "Come here, we have to talk to them!"

Inside, everyone's standing in a loose circle, talking, but Piper and Kyle look up when we approach. Dani's been my friend for years, but Piper and Kyle are new as of last year. Piper is in Dani's history class and Kyle was my science partner last year. I'm still getting used to having a defined friend group (it's been just me and Dani for a long time), but it's been nice. And I think I can trust them to be nice to Makayla. Piper *loves* cats (much to my dismay), so they'll probably get along.

"Hey, guys," I say hurriedly, "I convinced Makayla to join Sunshine Club, but she's super shy and so I thought—"

"Slow down!" Piper laughs. She moves her brown hair out of her face. Piper is a little shorter than me and she always wears black nail polish. She used to wear lots of goth clothes but she said she got tired of doing that much makeup every morning. She likes the nail polish, though, so she's always keeping her nails black and shiny. "You're always going so fast, Janie!"

"Who's Makayla?" Kyle asks. Kyle's the tallest out of all of us, after his growth spurt a few months ago. And his voice is super deep now too! Dani always tells me she wants to steal his new voice because it's "undeniably cool." I think it's kind of funny, because it doesn't really fit Kyle. He's so sweet and soft-spoken, so it's surprising to hear a deep voice coming from him.

"JV's new sister," Dani says. She turns to me, eyebrows raised. "She's shy?"

"Yeah. So, I was hoping we could all be friends with her. Like, make sure she's—"

"Of course, Janie! We're not gonna be mean to your sister, god." Piper laughs again as she cuts me off.

I can't stop myself from shooting a half glare at Piper. If I'm honest, Piper is my least favorite of the group. She always talks over me and treats everything like a joke. But I can't tell Dani that; gotta keep the peace. Being nice is not the same thing as being Makayla's friend, and Piper knows it. But I don't get a chance to correct her, because Makayla nervously peeks into the clubroom.

"Hey, Makayla! Come here." I wave her over and she reluctantly approaches. She looks even more scared now than she did earlier in math class. "These are my friends, Dani, Kyle, and Piper."

Makayla waves at them a little, but she doesn't have to talk. Piper and Kyle are already introducing themselves, and Dani happily starts explaining the Sunshine Club activities. I don't say anything, but when Makayla looks overwhelmed, I reach for her hand. She jumps a little, but then shoots me a grateful look out of the corner of her eye and squeezes my hand so tight it might fall off. I squeeze back. Piper is really talkative and Kyle is too, when you get him started on Dungeons & Dragons, but I hope they can be her friends. I hope she won't be nervous around them for long.

"Okay, okay, everyone settle down!"

I look up and our advisor, Mrs. Clarity, is waving everyone

over. She's a nice white lady with really sharp green eyes. She's super into volunteering, and she's the owner of Buttons.

"We're headed to the nursing home today! Oh, a new member?" Mrs. Clarity looks at Makayla in surprise, who practically hides behind me to get away.

"This is Makayla, my st—my new sister." I smile at her and she smiles back. "She wants to try out the club."

"Oh, wonderful! Welcome, Makayla!" Mrs. Clarity is so excited she's practically vibrating. "Do you like dogs? Buttons absolutely loves new club members. Oh wait, first—" Mrs. Clarity clears her throat. "I have an announcement: Though we've loved Alice's leadership over the past semester, she's asked to step down as president to focus on her studies."

I frown. Alice was one of the founding members . . . and she's done? Just like that? I whip my head around to see Alice blushing and ducking her head. Wait, if Alice isn't in charge, then that means—

"That means we need a new president!" Mrs. Clarity grins.

I look at Dani wildly, and her mouth is hanging open. How

many times have we talked about this?! Presidential election! The Sunshine Club we built from nothing, and I could be the president!

Mrs. Clarity keeps talking, even though all I can hear is excited buzzing in my ears. "Since we have some new members, let's delay the elections for a month, to give everyone a chance to get to know the candidates. How fun!"

Fun is right! Dani beams at me as Mrs. Clarity goes over the usual rules for visiting the nursing home. This is it. This is my chance. Something small and urgent stirs in my chest. Sunshine Club is the best thing I've ever done, and I can't wait to run for president.

Makayla squeezes my hand again, startling me. She gives me a shy smile and mouths "Good luck!"

I can't help but smile back.

Chapter 4

Lula gives me a big hug as soon as we get to the nursing home. She smells like lavender and mothballs, which I've really come to like over the past year.

"Janie, baby! How's my favorite?"

"Good." I hug Lula back before we break apart and sit at the small card table the nursing home set up for us. Lula is my favorite too, though I can't tell the other residents. Lula is a super short Black lady and her back curves downward a bit, but she won't ever use a cane like the nurses beg her to. She's eighty-nine years old and she told me she remembers when TV didn't have colors. Which is, like, whoa. She tells me all kinds of interesting stories, but she refuses to talk to anyone except me or Dani. The other residents say she's just cranky, but she told me once I look just like her granddaughter, who is now forty-five. I *think* that's a compliment.

Lula busies herself with setting up a game of checkers. She moves really slowly, probably because she's eighty-nine, but I don't mind waiting. More time to talk, and less time for her to beat me in checkers. She never lets me win.

Buttons barks happily, startling me. He's playing with a ball Kyle threw and three residents are crowding around, watching. "Do you want to try playing with Buttons today?" I ask.

"What? You want me to play with that mutt? Heck no." Except, she doesn't say "heck."

I sigh, laughing. Lula hates dogs almost as much as I hate cats. Oh well, I tried. "Okay, okay. We can play checkers again."

"Good," Lula grunts. "Now, tell me something new."

A burst of excitement fills my whole body. "There's going to be a presidential election! For Sunshine Club!"

"Oh?" Lula smiles, her eyes wrinkling so much I can barely see them. "It's rare for you to look so happy, Janie."

"I know, I know. But I'm really excited! Dani and I built the club, but we were too young to run for president last year. So this year . . . !"

Lula nods, still smiling. "Are you and Dani both running for president?"

I pause, unsure. I hadn't thought to ask her if she wanted to run too. "We'll talk about it."

Lula nods again. She carefully starts putting our checkers on the board. "You'll work it out. You're good friends."

I glance at Dani out of the corner of my eye. She's happily chatting to her favorite resident, an old man named Reggie. They play poker together all the time. She wouldn't run against me, would she? But . . . we did start the club together. Maybe that's the way it should be. I wouldn't mind if Dani was president—I could be VP! I return my attention to Lula. "Yeah, I think it'll be okay."

Lula finally finishes setting up the game. "Now, election aside, isn't there something else?"

I glance at Makayla this time. She's hanging out with Piper, who's talking to a group of residents. She's not saying much and still looks really nervous. "Yeah. I missed last week because I have a new st—a new sister."

"How's that going?"

I shrug. "Pretty good, I think. I like her, but she's really shy." I hesitate, then cave. "But it's kinda hard to get everyone on our schedule. We were so early for school today. And Makayla got to the bathroom first, so I was late for breakfast."

"Oh lord, Janie." Lula shakes her head as she moves her piece toward my side of the board. "You're the only kid I know who would complain about being early somewhere."

"That's not it! We have a schedule and we have to stick to it—"

Lula rolls her eyes. "You talk like you're seventy years old, you know that? Live a little! Be spontaneitous."

"Be what?"

"Bah, you know what I mean." She waves a captured red piece at me. She's already beating me! "It's good to follow the rules, but it's bad if you're not flexible. Listen to me, Janie. I got eighty years on ya."

"Okay," I grumble. I try to focus on the game, but I can't shake Lula's warning. I have to adhere to the schedule. I have to. Bad things happen if we don't. Lula doesn't get that.

We play quietly for a while. I always have to really concentrate when we play because she's ruthless! Lula pauses for a second, considering her next move. I've lost six of my pieces already . . .

Lula clears her throat. "Don't be upset. If it makes you happy, you can be on your schedule. And if your sister hogs the bathroom, I'll beat her up."

I laugh. The schedule isn't about happiness, but I am happy Lula would defend me. I can't imagine wanting to beat up Makayla though.

"Okay, Lula. Thanks."

She smiles and we play checkers until our peaceful hour is up.

We're an hour and thirty-eight minutes late for dinner.

Everything that could have gone wrong did. First, after

Sunshine Club was over, Makayla and I waited on Mom for *thirty minutes*. I'm so upset! Mom knows I have Sunshine Club every Monday and Thursday. Every day for a year and a half! And if she forgot, it's on the calendar in the kitchen. She was really sorry, and I thought it might be okay and we'd still make dinner, but then Keisha was late because she got a call from the fire station. When has Lavender Falls ever had a fire?! I reminded Mom we have homework and bedtime, but she wanted to eat dinner with everyone, so we had to wait on Keisha. Then I didn't know what to do. I can't do my homework until after we have dinner. But now we're so late, I'll have to rush to do my homework and I'll probably go to bed later than I always do. I'm so frazzled, as Lula says. This family is killing me.

I sit at the table, in a terrible mood, while Mom and Keisha chat happily in the kitchen. Makayla sits next to me, sighing. At least she's on time.

"Mom? Are you almost ready?"

"Ready!" Mom finally brings in several McDonald's bags.

She sits them in the middle of the table. "Not exactly gourmet, but it'll do, right?"

I'll eat anything right now. I'm starving. I don't wait for Makayla; I pull out my chicken nuggets with BBQ sauce right away. She waits for me to get done before pulling a burger out of the same bag.

Keisha brings bottles of water for everyone and we're all finally sitting at the table. "How was school, girls?" she asks.

I start to answer, but Makayla beats me to it. "Oh, it was wonderful!"

Wonderful? She seemed so nervous all day, even at Sunshine Club.

Keisha seems to brighten. "Really? How are your classes? Did you make new friends?"

"They're great! My teachers are so nice, and Janie introduced me to her friends, and they're really nice too." Makayla gives me a grateful smile, and she looks way happier than I've ever seen her.

My friends *are* nice, but I didn't really see her hanging out with anyone . . . I put down my nuggets and listen to Makayla describe her day. Most of it is true, but she's putting a real positive spin on things. She doesn't mention the disaster in math class, or that she didn't actually speak to Dani, Piper, or Kyle. And Keisha seems happier and happier the more Makayla talks.

Makayla gets done with her story and Keisha still looks happy. "I'm so glad, Makayla! It really seems like you're adjusting well! Let me know if anything happens, okay?"

"Okay," Makayla says. I'm watching her closely, so I don't miss the flash of relief that crosses her face.

"What about you, Janie?" Mom asks, smiling at me. She's already done with her fish sandwich. "How was school?"

"Fine." I put down the last of my french fries. I'll think about Makayla later; this is important. "But I think we need to talk about the schedule."

Mom laughs and I automatically prickle. "I'm sorry I was late today, Janie. I'll do better tomorrow."

"No, tomorrow I walk home because I don't have Sunshine Club. You know that, Mom!" I don't understand. She was so good about following the schedule . . . until Keisha and Makayla moved in.

"Sorry, sorry." Mom is still laughing. "If you're walking home, what about Makayla?"

I blink for a second, shocked. Oh no. I haven't planned for Makayla at all! What does she want to do after school? Will she come to Dani Time with me? But I like to hang out with Dani alone . . .

"Just relax, Janie," Mom says. She glances at Keisha and her smile softens, just a little bit. "Everything will be much easier now that Keisha's here. You'll see."

I don't say anything, since Mom and Keisha are looking at each other in that gross couple way. I sigh and push away from the table. Mom says things will be easier, but easier for who?

Chapter 5

After I take a shower, I freeze in the doorway of my bedroom.

Pumpkin is in my room.

The cat sniffs at my dirty clothes pile, long tail twitching. I don't move, my heart in my throat. She's in my room! How did she get in here?! How do I get her to go away?

"Okay, Pumpkin," I say, easing to my bed to get my pajamas. "Stay right there. Don't move."

Pumpkin ignores me. She abandons my clothes and bats a fallen pencil around under my desk. This is good! If she's distracted, she can't hurt me. I change into my pajamas like lightning, never taking my eyes off Pumpkin. She's still playing with the pencil so she doesn't notice me changing.

Okay, I'm in my pajamas . . . but now what? Pumpkin gets bored with the pencil and flops down on my clothes from earlier. Right between me and the door. Ugh.

"Pumpkin, please," I can't help but whine. "Please leave. Maybe Makayla will give you a treat?"

Pumpkin's ears twitch at the word *treat*. She looks at me, her green eyes round.

"Wait, no! Not from me!"

Pumpkin gets to her feet, tail twitching.

"No, I don't have any treats!"

Pumpkin meows at me, and to my horror, trots toward me. Panic hits me all at once—she's gonna scratch me! I barely hold in a scream as I scramble onto my bed.

"This is the worst," I groan. Pumpkin meows loudly, moving in circles below me like a shark. "This is why I hate cats. A dog wouldn't torture me like this. This is so unfair."

Pumpkin sits down, staring at me intently. Maybe she'll

realize I don't have any treats and leave me alone. Maybe she'll never leave and I'll die up here on my bed of dehydration. Too early to tell.

"Pumpkin?" Makayla's muffled voice calls from the hallway. "Where are you?"

I'm so happy I could cry. "She's in here! In my room! Hurry!"

I'm so relieved when Makayla pushes my door open. She frowns at me. "Janie? What're you doing?"

I point to Pumpkin, who's sitting right under me. "Your cat's right here."

Makayla gasps and runs to my bedside. She scoops Pumpkin into her arms, holding the cat like a baby. I can't even move, I'm so shocked. Whoa. Pumpkin isn't scratching or biting or anything. She's just lying in Makayla's arms, her eyes half-closed. Makayla is some kind of cat whisperer.

"I'm so sorry! I thought she was downstairs. You can come down now."

"It's okay." It's not, but it's not her fault. I need to remember to close my door all the way. I wish I didn't *have* to do that . . . but whatever. I won't think about it. I hop off my bed and face Makayla. "Thanks for rescuing me."

"No problem. But she's really nice!" Makayla says. "She won't hurt you, I promise. Do you want to pet her?"

Maybe Pumpkin won't hurt *her*, but she doesn't know me. "Umm, that's okay. I don't want to take any chances." I hurry to continue because Makayla seems a little sad. "How was Sunshine Club today? I'm sorry I didn't get a chance to talk to you much at the nursing home."

"Oh, it was good." Makayla shifts Pumpkin in her arms. Pumpkin just closes her eyes. "Your friends are really nice, Janie. You're lucky."

Lucky? That's kind of weird to say about friends, isn't it? "They're pretty nice. Do you think you'll join for real?"

Makayla hesitates, not looking at me at first. But then she meets my eyes and gives me a shy smile. "I think so. I really love volunteering. And you'll be a good president for sure."

My chest swells with happiness. "Thank you! I'm so excited to run! I have a bunch of really cool ideas—" I stop myself before I start rambling. "Well, I can tell you about them in the club on Monday. But bedtime now!"

Makayla seems a little baffled. "Oh, uh, right now? I was gonna ask you about some of the math homework."

"Sorry," I say. "But it's bedtime, according to the schedule." Actually, it's past bedtime, thanks to the late dinner and Pumpkin incident, but I'll keep that to myself.

Makayla still seems confused, so I add, "The main schedule is in the kitchen, but I can show you the one I have here."

"Oh, uh, that's okay." Makayla moves to the door and smiles tentatively. "I'll go to bed now. See you tomorrow."

I wave and close my door after her. I'm late for bedtime, but only by twenty minutes. Not so bad! Better than dinner anyway. I'm so busy brushing my teeth, wrapping my hair, and triple-checking my door is closed and locked, I don't have time to think about Makayla until after I'm in bed.

I frown at my dark ceiling. What exactly does "lucky" mean?

And why was she so shy with me just now, but so energetic at dinner? But maybe it's none of my business. Maybe I just need to focus on how to make sure all of us stay on schedule, not just for me, but for everyone's sake. I heave a sigh and close my eyes. Tomorrow, I'll get to work.

Chapter 6

I ride my bike to the skatepark after school the next Tuesday.

Dani waves at me, waiting at the front gate. She has her rainbow helmet in one hand and skateboard in the other.

"JV!" She sings as I arrive at the gate. "It's Dani Time!"

I roll my eyes, trying to hold back a laugh. "I wish you'd stop calling it that."

"That's what you called it first!"

She's not wrong. When I first started my schedule, I made a lot of mistakes. Number one being that I didn't budget time for Dani. She got upset when we were in fifth grade, and we had a big fight about it. I felt bad, so I wrote in my planner "Dani Time" every Tuesday and Friday after school. She saw my planner once and thought it was really funny, and she's been teasing me about it ever since.

Dani Time has changed a lot over the years since I first put it in my schedule. Dani always picks what we do and where we go, so I've been bowling, to a knitting class and an acting class, and one week we even tried this horrible workshop about pickling vegetables. Thankfully we quit that one really quick. Dani says, in her quest for "peak coolness," she has to be well-rounded. I don't know how that'll make her cooler, but I don't complain. Lately, Dani's been into skateboarding and since I have a bike, we hang out at the skatepark every Tuesday and Friday, 3:30 to 5:30. This is one Dani Time activity I like.

Dani and I walk into the park together. No one's here; it's pretty cold out, so that makes sense. But Dani wants to skateboard, so we're both here.

"I'm gonna do a kickflip today," Dani says, her voice burning with determination. "Are you doing any tricks?"

"No. I like all my bones unbroken."

Dani giggles and I smile too. I admit doing tricks on my bike would probably be fun, but I need to think. My life has suddenly become a lot more complicated than it used to be.

I watch Dani do some tricks on her board for a while, and then I ride my bike around the track of the park. It's kind of peaceful, even if it's cold, so I'm glad Dani picked the skatepark. I try to think about a new schedule, and the election, and Mom's increasing slipups on our current schedule, but it all blends together and I can't think of anything. So, I just ride around for a while, waiting for Dani to get done. After Dani Time is over, then it's dinner, and then homework, then beg Makayla to get Pumpkin out of my room (Mom *always* forgets to close my door), and then bed. And it would all work out if everyone followed the schedule, but they're all so bad at it! We're late for dinner every night and early for school every day. Everything is a mess.

I get tired of riding and I sit next to Dani. She grins at me. "What're you thinking, JV? You look really mad."

"I'm not mad." I cross my arms and sigh. "I'm just stressed. My schedule is all messed up."

"I keep telling you not to take that schedule so seriously!"

"I *have* to, Dani. That's the only way things will work out."

"They're not working out now?"

"No! Everything is awful. We're too early for school, and then Mom has been forgetting to pick us up on the days we have Sunshine Club, and then Keisha is always so busy at the firehouse. And it's kind of unrelated, but Makayla's cat keeps trying to sneak into my room. It's a nightmare. My stomach hurts."

Dani frowns at me, leaning back on her hands. "Sounds like that's not your schedule, Janie."

I meet her eyes. "What do you mean?"

"Like, your mom shouldn't forget to pick you up. That's not cool."

"That's what I'm saying! She needs the schedule. If we don't have it, everything goes so bad."

"Okay, that's fair. It's probably hard to adjust to two new people. But what about Pumpkin?"

"The cat?" Dani nods and I blink in confusion. "I don't like cats and she's making me miserable, but what does that have to do with Mom?"

"Why did your mom let a cat move into your house if she knows you don't like them? That's so mean."

"She just forgot . . ."

"Janie."

I wince. Dani doesn't like my mom very much, because of what happened pre-schedule. But she's doing so much better now! Well, she was. Before she got married anyway. "Can we talk about something else?"

Dani sighs, but nods. "Okay. How is Makayla? I don't see you talking to her much at school."

I pause, some of the hurt getting replaced with confusion. Maybe Dani can help me figure this out. "Actually, I've noticed something weird about her."

"Yeah?"

"So at school, she's really shy, right? Doesn't talk much. But at home, she tells Keisha she's making lots of friends and having fun."

Dani's eyebrows furrow. "Why would she lie?"

"It's not really a lie." I pause, thinking about how happy Piper seemed yesterday when she found out that Makayla likes the same band she does, the Glitter Bombs. "But I don't know why she's trying so hard to convince Keisha."

"Hmm. That is weird. But I guess it doesn't hurt anything, right?"

Yeah, that's true. I'm just confused about it. I really want to talk with her more, like Dani and I do, but I'm so stressed about the schedule and the election, I haven't really had time. Maybe tonight (if we have dinner on time), we can talk. I like the Glitter Bombs too.

"Anyway," Dani says, standing up and grabbing her board. It has a new sticker on the bottom, I'm just noticing. It's a yellow, white, purple, and black flag. Dani is really particular about what stickers are on her board, so I'm curious what this one means. So far, only Raichu from *Pokémon* and Steph Curry's basketball number have made the cut. "If it gets too much, just run away from home, yeah?"

I laugh and Dani does too. "Yeah. Great idea." I point to her board. "What's your new sticker?"

Dani gasps and flips the board over so I can see. "Oh my god, I forgot to tell you. It's an enby flag!"

"Oh, cool!" Dani told me she's nonbinary last year. *Enby* is short for the letters *N* and *B*, for *nonbinary*. I didn't get it at first, but she explained it like this: She doesn't feel like a girl, but she doesn't feel like a boy either. It's like gender is on two sliding scales, one that's masculine, one that's feminine, that go from 0 to 100. Some people feel 100 percent feminine and 0 percent masculine, but Dani feels maybe 65 percent feminine and sometimes 50 percent masculine. So that's why she asked me to use *she/they* pronouns. "I like it! Where'd you get it?"

"At Hastings, where I got my board. They have all kinds of cool stuff." Dani pauses, fiddling with the white wheels on her skateboard. She doesn't look at me. "I'm thinking about coming out to my mom and dad."

I stay quiet, studying her face. I don't think her parents would react badly, but I don't know. I'm the only one who knows she's nonbinary. Dani said she's afraid to tell anyone else, so I haven't told anyone either, and I only use *she/her* pronouns at school. But I support her by using *they* whenever I talk about her with Mom or Keisha. Even if they figure it out, they won't be jerks about it or blab to Dani's parents. "Do you want me to come with you?"

"I'm not telling them today!" Dani looks up and smiles. "But soon. I think I just gotta do it, you know? Like ripping off a Band-Aid."

"Yeah. But only when you're ready." I scoot closer to her. "And I'll be there with you if you want me to."

"Thanks, JV. You're awesome." Dani suddenly stands, patting her cheeks. "This is too serious! Wanna see me ride that railing?"

I laugh and stand too. "I have 911 on standby."

Dani and I ride around for another hour, and then we walk home together. Her house is just a few streets from mine, so it's never a big deal. When we get to her house, Dani skips to her porch.

"Sure you don't wanna come in?" Dani asks. "I've got the new *Resident Evil* game! Dad got it for me, but don't tell Mom. She'll freak out."

Oh man, I love that game. I can't play it alone because it's so scary . . . I really want to, but I shake my head. "I can't, sorry. Dinnertime, and then homework."

"Okay," Dani says, smiling. "Pencil it in on that planner! I'll wait for you."

I smile back. "Maybe after the election."

"Deal!"

I wave at Dani and head home. I walk beside my bike, deep in thought. Dani Time is over, and I have to move on to the rest of my day, but sometimes I really wish I could do something I didn't plan for. But I can't; I have to stay on schedule, no matter what. Even if it sucks sometimes. I heave a sigh and walk home, wishing I was at Dani's house instead.

Chapter 7

For once, we're not late for dinner!

I breathe a sigh of relief when I walk into my house and Mom, Keisha, and Makayla are here. Mom and Keisha are in the kitchen, and Makayla's waving a fish on a string in front of Pumpkin's face.

"Hi, Janie!" Mom sings.

"Hey, Mom." I close the door and wave to Makayla. She waves back, but that means Pumpkin isn't distracted anymore. She meows and starts trotting toward me. Ugh, why is this cat so interested in me?! I flee to the kitchen, where I can stand on a chair if I need to.

"Where've you been?" Keisha asks. She's actually out of her uniform today, which is amazing! I've never seen her without her boots. Now she's wearing some pink old-lady slippers.

"Dani, right?" Mom says.

"Yep!" She remembers! Dani is wrong; Mom just needs to get back on her schedule and she'll be fine. "Every Tuesday and Friday I hang out with my friend after school. Their name is Dani."

"Oh, that's so nice!" Keisha says. "I love that you make time for your friends, Janie."

I can't think of anything to say to that. I guess it is nice, but I like hanging out with Dani too. "Umm, yeah. What's for dinner? Can we eat on time?"

"Yes, ma'am, we can!" Mom picks up a spatula, grinning. "I'm cooking dinner tonight! We've been eating way too much takeout lately."

Oh no. Mom is a terrible cook. But that's fine, I can help.

"I can—"

"I'll help you," Keisha says at the same time.

I just blink at her for a second. But I . . . I always help Mom cook. I have to, because she burns toast. I look to Mom for help, but she's not looking at me. She's looking at Keisha, her smile so big I almost can't see her eyes.

"Thanks, Keisha! You know I'm so bad at this."

Oh. Mom doesn't want me to help. Unfamiliar hurt stabs my chest, so much it's painful. I wander out of the kitchen, my hand on my chest. It's good that Mom has help with cooking, which is what I wanted, but I guess I always thought the person who helped her would be me.

I go upstairs and sit at my desk. I kind of feel like going to bed early . . . but no! I can't go to bed, I have work to do. I pat my face with my hands to pump myself up. I need to find a way to win the election! Mrs. Clarity said it wasn't a big deal, but it is to me. I pick up my pencil to start writing down ideas when a blur of orange catches my eye. Crap, I forgot to close the door—

It's too late. Pumpkin waltzes into my room, tail straight up in the air. She stops by my desk and meows, rubbing her face against the legs of the chair.

"Ugh, Pumpkin, *please.*" I groan and pull my legs to my chest so she can't scratch them. "Go away! Go find Makayla."

She doesn't go away. She paws at my untied shoelace, her eyes big and round. They'd be really cute on a dog, but on a cat they're a little scary.

I hear footsteps and I'm relieved when Makayla appears at the top of the stairs. She smiles and picks up Pumpkin, who meows in protest.

"Sorry, Janie. She really likes you!"

"The feeling is not mutual," I mutter under my breath. I don't think Makayla hears me because she's petting Pumpkin, trying to hush her loud yowls.

"Shh, it's okay," Makayla says, bouncing Pumpkin like a

baby. And somehow, it works. Pumpkin stops yelling and starts purring as Makayla scratches behind her ears. I just don't know how she does it.

"How'd you do that?"

"Do what?"

I gesture at Pumpkin. "You just pick her up like it's nothing. And she doesn't even scratch you."

"Pumpkin's sweet. She won't scratch anyone! Well, unless you touch her belly. She hates that."

Belly off-limits, roger that. I'm burning that into my memory so I can somehow live through this without dying.

"Thanks for rescuing me," I say, sighing a little. "I was trying to work on the election stuff, but she distracted me."

"Oh, what kind of election stuff?" Makayla inches closer, peeking over my shoulder. "I could help, maybe? I'm free after school tomorrow."

Oh. I would like her to help, but tomorrow is Wednesday. On Wednesdays I hang out with Piper and Kyle . . .

Makayla's face falls. "No?"

"No, it's not that! I do want your help, but the election isn't on the schedule. That's why it's so hard."

Makayla frowns. "I've been hearing a lot about a schedule . . ."

"Let me show you!" I pull my planner out of my backpack and open it to this week. Every square of the calendar is color coded and scribbled on with notes. It's my pride and joy, even if I know the schedule by heart. "On Wednesdays I hang out with Piper and Kyle after school. And Tuesdays and Fridays I hang out with Dani. That's where I was today. But see? There's no room for the election."

Makayla blinks at the schedule several times. She puts Pumpkin down, and the cat wanders to my dirty clothes pile and flops to her side. "Umm, Janie . . ."

"Yeah?"

"Uh, nothing. It's just . . . super detailed."

My chest swells with pride. "Thank you! I worked really hard on it, you know. Hey, do you want one? I made Mom's too."

"I'm good," Makayla says.

"Oh, okay." I stare at the planner, looking at my week. "I've got it! Weekends are Family Time. Maybe we can hang out then?"

Makayla shakes her head. "I can't this weekend. I go to my dad's. But next weekend I can."

I'd almost forgotten about the mysterious Dad! I so want to ask her about him . . . would that be rude? Maybe, but I have to know. "Hey, about—"

"Girls!" Keisha's voice bellows from downstairs. "Dinner!"

Makayla brightens and scoops up Pumpkin. The cat growls, which makes me tense up, but Makayla isn't fazed. "I hope it's pork chops! Mom's so good at those."

She leaves, carrying Pumpkin downstairs, and I close my planner. I check my watch—ten minutes early for dinner. I'll take it. I follow Makayla, thinking that I somehow, someway, need to add Makayla Time to my already full schedule.

Chapter 8

After the last class, I head to Piper's locker.

It's Wednesday, so we all hang out together after school. Piper and Kyle aren't like Dani; we do the same thing every week, which is play Dungeons & Dragons. I don't . . . really like it. But, it's not fair for me to hang out with Dani and never hang out with them, so I just play along. Sometimes it's not so bad. It's fun making up stories, when Kyle isn't too intense about it. And we cheat a lot. Our party always makes it through the campaign.

Piper waves at me as I approach. "Janie! Perfect timing!"

"Yeah?" I adjust my backpack a little. This time, I came prepared. Piper and Kyle make fun of me for not knowing the game really well, so I thought about the campaign all through math. "I was thinking about how to get past the poison forest, and—"

"Let me stop you right there," Piper says. "I can't play D&D today."

I blink at her. But . . . but today's Wednesday. We always play on Wednesdays. "I . . . what do you mean? Why not?"

"I'm hanging out with Makayla! She's never heard of *Fruits Basket*. Can you believe it?"

I can believe it, because I've never heard of *Fruits Basket* either. "But what about the game?"

"We can do it on Friday or something!"

No, Friday is Dani Time. I guess I could ask Dani if she wants to join, but last time she played she didn't really like it, and Dani always picks what we do on Tuesdays and Fridays. "No, Piper, we always play on Wednesdays—"

"Lighten up, Janie," Piper says, laughing. She's already walking away from me. "You can handle one day without D&D. See you next week!"

I'm speechless as Piper skips away. We always play on Wednesdays. Always. For a whole year. My stomach twists and groans at the thought of the schedule falling apart. I hold my middle as I watch Piper meet Makayla at the end of the hall. Makayla waves shyly and Piper starts talking enthusiastically. I know it's not Makayla's fault, but I can't help but feel stung. She's here for two weeks and already wrecking the schedule.

No, I can't think like that. I'm sure this was Piper's idea and not Makayla's. Piper always laughs at my schedule. And anyway, it's good that Makayla is getting to know Piper. Maybe she can join D&D on Wednesdays, after they do the *Fruits Basket* thing, whatever it is. And then Makayla and I can have fun together, and I won't have to create a separate Makayla Time! This is actually great, if I think about it. One afternoon off schedule today, a future schedule that's even stronger later. My stomach pain eases and I nod to myself as I leave school, a whole hour and a half early. I'm glad they're hanging out, but . . . what am I going to do in place of D&D?

I ride my bike home, feeling kind of lost. Maybe I can work on election stuff. Or do homework? No, homework time is after dinner. What should I do? I don't feel so good about this free time. I haven't had free time in a long time.

When I get home, Mom looks up from her sketch pad. She's sitting on the couch, next to Pumpkin (who's thankfully asleep).

"Janie! What're you doing here?"

I close the door behind me. "D&D got canceled. So I came home early."

"Where's Makayla?"

I hesitate. It really doesn't sound good saying it out loud. "She's the reason it got canceled. Piper wanted to hang out with her today instead."

Mom blinks in surprise, then smiles at me. It's a soft, gentle one. "Come, sit down. Let's have a chat."

I glance at Pumpkin, who's awake now and looking at me right back. "Can you move the cat?"

65

Mom laughs. "Come on, Janie! You've got to be used to her by now, right? You're the one who was begging for a pet!"

A dog. *A dog.* She knows I wanted a dog! I take a deep breath to calm myself. "I don't want to sit next to the cat. Can you move it?"

Mom's smile falters, but just for a second. "Okay! Let's go in the kitchen. I'll get us some snacks."

I follow Mom to the kitchen, feeling kind of rotten. I don't want to be mad at her, or Makayla, but I'm not feeling so good. "Mega-stressed," Kyle called it once. When my schedule gets off, everything gets so bad. My stomach still hurts, and now I have an awful headache.

Mom grabs two bags of chips—plain for her and salt and vinegar for me. She might not remember what kind of pet I like, but at least she remembers this. "How has everything been? With Makayla and Keisha?" she asks.

I shrug, nibbling at the edge of a chip. "Okay."

"Just okay?" When I shrug again, Mom frowns. "Do you like Keisha?"

It's a little late for that question now, isn't it? She's married to her and Keisha lives in our house. "She's fine. It's not that I don't like them, it's just that they throw us off our routine."

"It's not just *our* routine now, though, Janie. Keisha and Makayla are part of our family too."

I fidget a little. I know she's right, but it doesn't really *feel* like it. Makayla talks to Keisha and I talk to Mom and that's it. Well, I guess Makayla talks to Piper too. And Pumpkin hangs around me annoyingly, like she's doing now. She's trying to rub her face against my ankles. Ugh.

"Just give it some time, okay? And give Keisha and Makayla a chance. Change is difficult for everyone, but especially Makayla. She had to change schools and friends, and she just needs a little grace from us right now."

Now I feel bad. Mom's right. I can give up one day of D&D for Makayla, who had to give up everything. I take a bite out of my chip and nod. "Okay, Mom. I will."

"Good!" Mom leans over and kisses the top of my head. "You're such a good girl, Janie. Now, since you're not with your friends, want to help me paint?"

I don't, but I nod anyway and we head to Mom's studio, which is just a tiny storage building in the backyard. And painting is a good distraction (especially when Mom throws paint at me and we get into a paint war), but there's a tiny thought in the back of my mind that I can't shake. Mom said things are hard for Makayla and Keisha, and I get that but . . . why didn't she say things might be hard for me too?

Chapter 9

When I sit at Lula's card table, I'm feeling pretty miserable.

I can't stop thinking about what Mom said, about things being hard for Makayla. And I get it, I really do, but I feel a really terrible feeling in my gut when I see her talking and laughing with Piper. Apparently, the *Fruits Basket* thing was a hit; that's all they talked about on the bus ride here. Even when I tried to join the conversation, Piper ignored me and kept talking about the "stunning animation." Makayla looked guilty, but she didn't stop Piper either. I just sat in silence until we got to the nursing home.

It doesn't look like things are hard for Makayla. It kind of looks like things are hard for me.

"Uh oh," Lula says, eyeing my face. "What happened? Who's being mean to my baby?"

"Nobody." I sigh. "Things are just not going well, Lula."

"This about that infernal schedule again?"

I wrinkle my nose. "Kind of. But not really. I'm just really tired."

"You too young to be tired!" Lula snorts. "But tell me what's going on. Not sleeping?"

"No . . ." I debate on telling her about Makayla, but decide against it. Makayla's sitting nearby, reading a magazine to one of the residents who doesn't have great eyesight. Buttons is sitting right in her lap too. I get a burst of jealousy, but stuff it back down. I can play with Buttons later. "See, Keisha is always late for dinner. And when she's late, that means I have to push my homework back because I always do my homework after dinner."

Lula raises her eyebrows, but doesn't say anything. Maybe she wants me to keep talking?

"And . . . and my friends canceled our game yesterday. We always play every Wednesday! I don't know what to do when we don't play, you know?"

Lula nods, still quiet. I hesitate. I don't want to tell her about what happened on the bus, even if Makayla wasn't sitting close by. It's just too much.

"Okay, Janie. Listen to Lula, okay?" Lula waits until I nod before continuing. "You gotta let that schedule go. You're a kid! You shouldn't be worrying about this stuff."

I shake my head. I can't let it go. She doesn't understand.

Lula sighs. "Okay. How about this. Why don't you try being more flexible?"

"What do you mean?"

"You said you don't do your homework until after dinner. Why not start while you're waiting?"

I shrug helplessly. "Dinner comes first, and then homework."

"Oh lord, kids these days are stubborn as mules—when your friends don't wanna hang around you, what do you do? Mope?"

I don't say anything. I did mope yesterday.

"Exactly! Make use of that time! Why not do something fun or relaxing? Something just for you."

I frown at the card table. I guess she's right. It doesn't make sense to not do *anything* on Wednesdays and while I'm waiting on dinner.

"Maybe," I say reluctantly. "But I'm sure Piper and Kyle will have D&D next week. So it won't matter. We'll get back on track soon."

Lula shakes her head. "Stubborn, stubborn, just like a little mule. You remind me of me."

I shift in my chair, fidgeting with two of my checkers. "Are you stubborn too?"

"Not stubborn. Always right." Lula gives me a conspiratorial wink. But then her expression gets really serious, and also a little . . . sad? "Janie, I've made some mistakes. I've been stubborn like you, and sometimes digging your heels in isn't the way to go. It can ruin everything."

I frown at Lula as she stares back at me. What does she mean? What ruined everything? "Lula—"

"Bah, enough of that!" Lula puts her last checkers on the board and motions for me to put mine down too. "Let's play. You'll listen to Lula soon enough, hmm?"

I smile at her, but I'm still feeling uneasy. I feel like Lula is trying to warn me about something, but what else can I do? I have to follow the schedule. I can't "be flexible" when there's so much at risk. She just doesn't get it.

Lula and I play checkers and she beats me (as usual) until it's time to go. I wave at her as we board the bus, but, for the rest of the day, I can't shake that uncomfortable feeling her words gave me.

Chapter 10

I've decided what to do about the election.

Mrs. Clarity hasn't said anything about campaigns, so I think I shouldn't go too far. But I still want to do something . . . So I'm thinking I'll make a quick speech and throw out some ideas, and that'll be it. And I'll also bring some cookies, because who wouldn't vote for someone who brought you free dessert?!

I rush down to the kitchen, taking the steps two at a time. Today's Sunday, which is the only day I don't have much planned. When it was just me and Mom, we'd sleep in until ten, and maybe paint together. But now . . . I shake my head to clear it. Now, I'm baking cookies. That's all.

I peek into the kitchen cautiously—no Pumpkin. Thank goodness. She's been terrorizing me all weekend because Makayla's at her dad's. Keisha said she's lonely, but that doesn't mean she can sleep in my room and potentially claw me in the middle of the night. Mom has had to carry her out of there three times already.

I go to the fridge and start pulling out the ingredients for cookies. I taught myself how to bake them two years ago, and then other stuff after that. I like baking a lot. But I don't do it much because Dani says it's boring and Piper and Kyle only want to eat the end product and not help me.

"Janie?"

I jump, almost dropping the eggs. Keisha's standing in the doorway of the kitchen, smiling at me.

"What're you up to?"

"Oh, umm, I'm baking cookies. Well, I have to make the batter first."

"Oh, that's so nice. Can I help?"

Help? But why? Cookies are pretty easy. They don't take that long. But Keisha looks kind of hopeful, so I feel bad saying no. Makayla's at her dad's and Mom is still sleeping. Keisha said Pumpkin was lonely, but maybe Keisha is too.

"Sure." I move my stepladder so she can get to the counter.

Keisha beams at me. She washes her hands and stands beside me. "What kind of cookies are we making? And what for?"

"Just chocolate chip. And they're for Sunshine Club." I pause, then add, "Actually, it's because I'm running for president. When everyone votes, maybe they'll remember how good these cookies are."

Keisha laughs and I smile too. Keisha has this big, booming laugh that scared me the first time I heard it. But I'm used to it now, I think.

"Genius! I like the way you think, Janie." Keisha reaches into the top cabinet and pulls down a bag of caramel chips. "Why not do chocolate and caramel cookies? That might be fun."

"Two different cookies? That's a lot of extra work."

"No! In the same cookie!"

I pause, considering it. I would have never thought of that. The recipe calls for just chocolate chips, and that's what I've made every time. But Keisha has that hopeful look again, and I *do* like caramel, so I nod. "Okay. Let's do it."

We start to make cookie dough, and I have to admit, it's more fun with someone else. Keisha asks me lots of questions, about how gooey I want the cookies to be, or if I think a little more sugar than the recipe says would hurt. Finally, when they're in the oven, we both wash our hands and sit at the kitchen table. Keisha scrapes the cookie dough bowl with a spoon and winks.

"Don't eat too much, but a little can't hurt, right?"

"Actually, you can get salmonella." I eat the cookie dough she hands me anyway. It's a lot sweeter than normal . . . were the caramel chips a good idea?

Keisha laughs again and eats her spoonful. "If we get sick, you can blame me." She looks at me then, her eyes soft and curious. "Now, while we wait, tell me about this Sunshine Club."

"Didn't Makayla tell you?"

"Yep. But I want to hear it from you."

Oh. I fidget in my chair, a little embarrassed. "It's a volunteer club. I made it! Well, it was already established, kind of, but there was only one member. So me and Dani—they're my best friend—we did lots of recruitment and stuff, and now we have ten members. No, eleven with Makayla!"

Keisha smiles. "It sounds really fun. You're proud of it."

"Yeah, I guess." But it's not a guess. I am really proud of Sunshine Club. I like going to skateparks, and painting, but I *love* Sunshine Club. I love cleaning things that have been forgotten, and playing checkers with Lula, and even just making cookies for the ten other people who like that too. It's the one place I don't have to pretend. "It's really a great club. And it fits perfectly in my schedule."

"That's another thing I've been hearing about. Janie's famous schedule." Keisha chuckles, but not like she's making fun of me. She sounds curious again. "Do you really have every day planned for the next year?"

"Yep, every day."

Keisha nods thoughtfully. "So what happens if something unexpected pops up?"

"I get a stomachache."

Keisha laughs again and I do too, but I'm not really kidding. I've had a stomachache since she and Makayla moved in with us.

"Okay, so tell me why you have such a strict schedule?"

I kick the toe of my shoe against the table. I don't think anyone except for Dani has ever asked. "I have to. Or bad things will happen."

Keisha frowns and I look down at the table so I won't have to meet her eyes. "What kind of bad things?"

I just shrug. The kitchen smells like sugar heaven. If the cookies are almost done, I won't have to answer her questions too much longer.

"You don't have to tell me," Keisha says. Her voice is soft and kind, so I look up at her. "The answer you gave me is enough. Gotta keep the schedule or bad things will happen. Roger that."

Well, now she makes me want to tell her! How does she do that?! This feels like a super OP adult skill. I need to make sure

I learn it when I grow up. I sigh, just a little. Maybe it won't hurt to tell her.

"So . . . you know Mom needs to take her medicine."

Keisha nods, frowning slightly. "I know."

"Well, before she met you, she was really bad at remembering to take it. And when she doesn't take it, she gets really forgetful. And sometimes she gets super excited about painting, and paints so much that she forgets to go to work. And sometimes she gets really sad and can't get out of bed."

I stop, staring at the table. This is kind of hard to talk about. I take a shaky breath.

"One day when I was in fourth grade, I came home from school and all our stuff was on the side of the road. Mom forgot to pay rent so the landlord got mad and locked us out." I take another breath. "We went to live with Grandpa, who was always yelling at us, and he had this awful cat that always scratched and bit me, and it was just horrible. S-so I—I thought if I made a schedule, a strict one, she wouldn't forget anything anymore. And it worked! She doesn't forget now. But I guess . . ." I trail off. I can't bear to think about what would happen if she got off the schedule again. I like our house. I don't want to go back to Grandpa's ever again. It's just too much.

Keisha surprises me when she reaches for my hand. I look up at her and she has a really serious expression on her face. "I'm sorry you went through that, Janie. You were really brave, and you did a great job."

My eyes are itchy and watery all of a sudden. I haven't cried in a long time, so I blink until my eyes are clear. "Thanks, Keisha."

"You're welcome. I'm really proud of you. But . . ." Keisha pats my hand gently. "If you can, I want you to try and not worry about your mom so much."

I frown at her. "I have to worry. Because lately she hasn't been staying on schedule, and then—"

"I know. But I think your mom is doing a lot better now. Plus, I'm here to help. I'll remind her of her meds, and I'll make sure she gets enough rest." Keisha looks right into my eyes, hers kind. "You don't have to parent your parent, Janie. It's okay to just be a kid and have fun. Let me take care of the adult things."

I can't say anything. What does she mean? I don't parent Mom . . . do I? I must look upset, because Keisha lets go of my hand and stands up. She gives me a big smile. "Just think about it, okay? No rush. For now, let's eat some cookies!"

Slowly, I stand up as Keisha puts on an oven mitt and takes the cookies out of the oven. She waves her hand over them and groans about how she can't wait to eat them. I almost want to laugh, but I don't feel so good. If Keisha takes over for Mom's schedule . . . what's my job? If Mom doesn't need the schedule anymore, what will I do?

Chapter 11

"Do you think it's cooler to play poker or blackjack?" Dani asks me as we walk into Sunshine Club.

"Neither. I like Go Fish."

Dani laughs and I smile. I'm holding the cookies Keisha and I made, and I'm feeling a little weird about our conversation still. But I've decided not to think about it, not yet. Election first, then think about Mom and the schedule.

"Janie!" Kyle says as soon as I enter the room. He grins, his eyes on the plate in my hands. "Is that what I think it is?"

"Yep! A different recipe this time though."

He reaches for one, but I pull it back. "Wait! I want to say something first."

"Say what?" Piper asks. She and Makayla are standing right next to each other. I don't know why, but I'm a little irritated by that. I had a good idea for the game last week and now I've forgotten it! Kyle's gonna make fun of me this Wednesday. But that's not Makayla's fault, not really, so I smile at them both.

"A little speech. About the election."

"A speech? Booo," Kyle says theatrically.

"Just a little one!"

"You know we're gonna vote for you." Piper isn't rolling her eyes, but her voice *sounds* like she is on the inside. "Skip the speech and give us cookies!"

"No cookies until you hear the speech!"

Everyone groans, but I stand at the front of the room anyway, and Mrs. Clarity helps quiet the group. I take a deep breath and say everything I practiced for hours after Keisha and I cleaned up the kitchen. It is really short.

"Anyway, I just want to say that I've really loved helping out this club. And I still remember when it was just me, Alice, and Dani—"

"And Alice barely helped us!" Dani yells. Everyone laughs and I do too.

"But if you vote for me, I'm sure we can make this club even better. New members, more effective volunteer opportunities at the nursing home, and maybe even more cookies."

Kyle cheers at the cookie part and I feel warm all over.

"Speaking of cookies, can we have some?" he says.

"Okay, okay." I pass out cookies to everyone, and we split into two groups: me, Dani, Makayla, Piper, and Kyle in one, the rest of the club members in the other.

"Oh my god, these are so good," Dani groans. She takes three more before I can say thank you. "You should be a baker. Like professionally."

"No way," Kyle says. "Janie's gonna be the president of the United States."

Honestly, being the president of the United States sounds like a lot of work. My schedule would be ridiculous. Maybe I'll see how being president of Sunshine Club is first.

"Hey, Janie," Piper says, wiping her hands on her napkin. "What did you mean by more volunteer opportunities at the nursing home? I was thinking that it's getting boring."

Boring? We're not volunteering to have fun . . . even if hanging out with Lula *is* really fun. I push away my irritation to answer her. "I don't think it's boring but I definitely think we should do something new. Like we have Buttons, but maybe we should get another dog to come with us. He can't be around everyone at once."

Piper wrinkles her nose. "Really? Buttons doesn't really do that much."

"The residents like Buttons—"

"But what does Buttons *do*?" Piper counters. "We need some variety. Something exciting!"

"What about a therapy cat?" Makayla suggests. She's speaking so softly I barely hear her.

Piper gasps. "That's genius! A dog and a cat! Variety!"

"Oh man, that would be awesome. Great suggestion!" Kyle says.

"You should run for president too," Piper teases. She looks at me and bursts into laughter. "Oh man, look at Janie's face! She's so mad!"

"I'm not mad," I argue, though I really am. Why would Piper say that?

Dani puts her arm around my shoulders. "Don't worry, JV. If a vicious kitty comes around, I'll beat 'em up for you."

Everyone laughs, except me. My good mood is all gone. When did my life get ruined by cats? Or really . . . when did Makayla get to be such a big problem?

I stare down Pumpkin with narrowed eyes. I'm on my bed and she's on the floor, lying on my dirty clothes pile. Mom left my door open *again*, so we're having a familiar standoff.

"What's so great about cats anyway?" I ask Pumpkin. She looks at me, her eyes half-closed. She blinks, really slowly.

"Seriously, why do people even like cats? Dogs are so much cooler. They can do tricks. What can you do?"

Pumpkin flops to her side, purring. Technically, I guess, that is something.

"Do you even know your name? Here, Pumpkin."

Her ears stick straighter and she rolls to her back, showing off her white, fluffy belly.

"All right, okay, that *is* pretty cute." I watch her roll all over my clothes for a while. I guess cats have some charm. They're pretty fluffy, and I bet some of the nursing home residents would love petting soft cat fur. Maybe Lula likes cats better than dogs? But cats scratch people; I would know. Pumpkin yawns, showing all her really sharp teeth. I shudder. Cats are just too risky.

Someone knocks on my door. It's got to be Mom—Keisha is still at work, and late for dinner, as usual. I really hate the "as usual."

"Come in. Everyone else is anyway," I add with a glare at Pumpkin. She ignores me and pads to the door, yowling.

Makayla peeks in, giving me a small smile. "Sorry to bother you, Janie."

"Oh, no problem." I nod at Pumpkin, who's now circling Makayla's legs. "I was just waiting for the cat to leave."

Makayla frowns a little. "Can I ask you something?"

"Yeah, sure."

"Were you upset earlier today? About bringing cats to the nursing home?"

I fidget, unsure what to say. The truth is yes, I am upset. I'm upset because I have no idea why everyone around me loves cats and I don't. I'm upset because Makayla just said my idea, but slightly different, and all my friends loved it. I'm upset because every day we eat dinner late, it pushes back my homework time and I sleep less, and I'm kind of cranky. I don't know.

I take a deep breath. None of this is Makayla's fault. "I'm okay. I was just surprised."

Makayla nods, still frowning. "Are you afraid of cats?"

I shrug, watching Pumpkin uneasily. "I just like dogs better. A lot better."

Makayla picks up Pumpkin, who meows in protest. "But you like Pumpkin, right? She's sweet."

I shrug again. I don't want to hurt her feelings, but we're getting dangerously close to me admitting I would love Pumpkin to be released into the wild and leave me in peace.

Makayla seems to make her mind up about something. "I know, you just need to get to know her better! You'll see."

And then, she does the worst thing anyone has ever done to me.

She puts Pumpkin on my bed.

I scream. I can't help it. I see Pumpkin, her fur fluffed up in surprise, right in scratching distance, and a scream rips out of my chest. Pumpkin's fur stands up even more and she scrambles off my bed and out the door as fast as her basketball-shaped body will go. I scramble to my feet, my heart in my throat, about to throw it up.

"Why would you do that?!" Now I'm screaming at Makayla. And she looks so stricken, so scared, I really wish I could calm down. But the cat was *right there*. In scratching distance! She could have really hurt me, and Makayla just—

"Janie . . . I'm really sorry." Makayla's voice is a fragile whisper. Her eyes are big and watery. "I didn't know you were that scared . . ."

I try to take a few deep breaths, but it's not really working. I scrub my face with the heels of my hands. "Can you—can you just leave me alone?"

It comes out way harsher than I mean. I just want to be by myself so I can calm down, but Makayla flinches like I've slapped her.

"Sorry," Makayla whispers again, and before I can say anything else, she leaves my room and closes the door behind her.

I sink down on my bed, my back against the wall. I hold my head in my hands until I can breathe okay again. I shouldn't have yelled at her, but why the heck did she do that?! She scared me, but now I feel bad about scaring her back. And Pumpkin. I don't like cats, but I didn't want to be mean to her. I look at my dirty clothes pile and a wave of sadness hits me. She'll probably avoid me now, and never come in my room again.

But wait, that's what I wanted! I don't want a cat in my room! And Makayla shouldn't scare me like that! It's mean! I'm already under so much stress because of the election and everyone loving her ideas and I'm starving but Keisha still isn't home . . .

I take a deep breath. This is time for an emergency contingency plan on my schedule: Go to bed early. I text Mom that I'm feeling sick and don't want dinner, turn off my light, and snuggle into my bed.

"It'll all be better in the morning," I whisper to myself. But I hardly sleep all night long.

Chapter 12

"Oh man," Lula says as I sit down at our card table. "What happened? Who hurt my baby?"

My throat burns like I'm about to cry, so I cough to clear it. Things were *not* better in the morning. I wanted to apologize to Makayla, but I woke up late and I was so frazzled, I forgot. And then things got super awkward, both at school and at home, and now I'm not sure how to talk to her. It's been two days! Two days and we haven't said anything to each other. I feel so bad, but also really mad at her for putting Pumpkin on my bed in the first place. The cat's been avoiding me since then too, and I hate to admit it, but I miss her rolling around on my floor.

But that's so much to tell Lula. Too much. I don't want to spend all our time focused on me. "I'm okay, Lula. It's nothing."

"Oh, so now we're lying?" Lula's thin eyebrows rise higher than I've ever seen. "That's not like you, Janie."

I fidget with the hem of my shirt, staring down at the card table. Everyone is having fun around me; Piper is laughing with Makayla and Kyle, Dani is playing cards with her buddy, and the upperclassmen are in a group, discussing something with the nurses. I feel like I'm the only one who's sad.

"Have you ever had to get along with a new family member?" I ask Lula.

Lula nods slowly. She hasn't moved to set up our usual game yet. "This is about your new sister, hmm?"

"Yeah. We got into a fight." I blink away the burn in my eyes. "I'm trying really hard, Lula, and nothing is working out. I don't know what to do."

Lula blows out a sigh. "Remember what I said about not being so stubborn and trying to be flexible?"

"Yeah, I know, but—"

"No buts." Lula sighs again. "Listen. I'll tell you a story. I've lived a long time, and I haven't lived perfectly. I'm here, aren't I?" Lula laughs, but it's quiet, bitter. "I have one daughter, Margaret. She's really wonderful; she went to school, something I couldn't do, got married, and now I have grandbabies and even great-grands. She's a great person and I'm proud of her. But I was stubborn, like you, and pushed her away. We said some things we can't take back, and we haven't spoken in years."

Pain curls under my ribs for her. I didn't know. Lula never talks about her family—I guess this is why.

"Don't be like me, little mule. Make up with your sister. You only have one family, and even though it's hard, you don't want to end up regretting it when you're old and gray."

"But I don't know how to . . ." I trail off, struck with inspiration. "Wait! What if I helped you talk to your daughter again?"

Lula's sad face turns into a scowl. "That wasn't the point of that story."

"I know, but I bet we can get your daughter to come and visit you! And you can apologize then."

"No."

"But maybe if we write a letter—"

"Janie." Lula's voice is so sharp, I flinch. She watches my face for a moment, then sighs heavily. "Well, all right. We can try it. But in exchange, you have to try and make up with your sister. Deal?"

"Deal!" I run to the front desk to grab some paper, an envelope, and stamps and run back. Lula and I spend the next twenty minutes writing Margaret a letter. It's fun, even though Lula argues with me about what to say.

"Tell her she can come to the senior karaoke night," Lula says. "She loves to sing. At least, she used to."

"When is it?" I write Lula's words carefully so I don't mess up. My handwriting really isn't that good. I didn't get the cute handwriting gene from Mom. I hope Margaret can read it.

"It's in two weeks, on Wednesday. Seven o'clock. You should come too. You like all them Disney songs."

I hesitate. Wednesdays are when I play ⌐ ⌐

done by 7:00 p.m. I'm sure Mom would take me if ..

and I would really like to meet Margaret . . . but no.

I shake my head. "I can't, Lula. It's not on the schedule."

Lula rolls her eyes. "You and that infernal schedule. Fine,

fine. Hurry up, finish that letter for me."

I do, and I add a PS at the bottom that I love Lula and it

would really mean a lot to her if she'd come. I have to hurry to

address the envelope to Margaret and put a stamp on it before

it's time for us to go, so it's not until I'm on the bus back to school

that I realize Lula seemed sad that I couldn't come to the kara-

oke night. Maybe it would mean a lot for me to come too.

I look out the window, unease and guilt twisting in my gut.

I wish I could go. I wish I could meet Margaret and tell her how

cool Lula is in person. I wish, just a little, that I didn't have to

have this schedule so things won't fall apart.

Mom is late picking us up. Again.

Dani's mom makes a sympathetic face at me as Dani climbs

ou girls need a ride home?"

, unsure, but I shake my head. Mom

ne Club. Every Monday and Thursday.

"N_____ ou, Mrs. Parona. Thanks for offering though."

"Okay . . ." Dani's mom seems hesitant, but climbs into her car.

"Bye, JV! Bye, Makayla!" Dani yells from the window. I wave as they drive away, and we're alone.

Makayla and I don't look at each other. I know I promised Lula I'd make up with her, but I don't know what to say. She wanted to talk to me earlier, but I messed up and now she won't talk at all. But honestly, that's really the least of my worries right now. I want to get home for dinner. On *time*. I want Mom to not be late picking me up, like she used to.

I check my watch. 5:40. Ten minutes late. I cross my arms against the cold. If she's too much later, Mrs. Clarity will come out of her office and demand to take us home. That's happened before, and it's so embarrassing.

"Umm, Janie?"

I look at Makayla in surprise. She wants to talk first? This is perfect! I clear my throat. "Umm, yes?"

Makayla wrings her scarf into a knot. "I wanted to talk to you."

"Oh, yeah. I'm sorry I blew you off on Tuesday, I just woke up late, and I hate that because it ruins the whole day . . ." I trail off. I shouldn't be talking so much. She's trying to apologize, I think. "Sorry, go ahead."

Makayla takes a shaky breath. "About Pumpkin . . . I didn't know you'd be so scared of her."

"Oh." That's not what I expected to hear. I start to tell her about Grandpa's cat, and that I secretly suspect all cats might be evil, but she hurries to continue.

"You said you weren't scared of cats. Pumpkin really didn't mean to scare you, Janie. She just wanted to play."

Play?! What?! No, she didn't—Makayla wanted her to. This isn't an apology at all! Indignation and something unfamiliar and sharp well up in my chest. "Well, I didn't want to play with her! I don't want to be around her at all."

Makayla's looking at me like she might burst into tears, and a wave of regret hits me. I shouldn't stay mad. She didn't know I don't like cats. I never even told her before now, so how could she? Mom's headlights shine on us as she speeds down the road, which puts me in a much better mood. I sigh heavily.

"Let's just forget it, okay?"

"Okay," Makayla says, her voice barely audible.

Mom pulls up beside us and waves at us cheerfully. "Taxi, at your service!"

"A late taxi!" Still, I climb into the back seat while Makayla gets in on the other side. "What happened?"

"Sorry, girls! I got caught up with painting. I'm working on this new piece and it's not quite right, but I think I'm close . . ."

I sigh and lean back against the seat. When Mom gets started talking about painting, she never stops. She talks about her new artwork the whole way home, until we get out of the car. I glance around, my stomach sinking. Keisha's car isn't in the driveway.

"Mom," I ask as she unlocks our front door, "where's Keisha?"

"Fire station," Mom says. "Another late night. But she'll be home soon!"

Another night, late for dinner. Great.

Mom and Makayla go to the living room. Mom's finally moved on from her painting to asking Makayla about Sunshine Club. Makayla answers, a little shyly. I wait for a little while, but Mom doesn't ask me anything. She doesn't even look at me.

I watch them talk, a little hurt. Everything has gotten way off track. It's silly, but I wish Mom would ask about my day too.

"I'm going upstairs while we wait," I tell Mom.

"Okay!" She goes right back to talking to Makayla. Makayla meets my eyes, but I look away.

I sit at my desk and lean back in my chair. 5:56. We should be eating in four minutes, but there's no way that's happening. How on earth can I get Keisha to come home on time? But . . . I know, in my heart, that's impossible. She can't just leave her job. I'll have to move dinnertime.

I'll have to change the schedule.

My stomach cramps at the thought. I groan and double over, pressing my face to my desk. I can't do it. I can't change the schedule, I just can't. Bad things happen when we change things, especially something as big as dinner. I can't. I can't do it.

But then I think about Lula, and how she encouraged me to be flexible. I stare at my planner, at the *Dinner: 6:00* sticker I put on every square of the calendar. I can't change dinnertime. It's too important. I'll have to find a way to get Keisha to come home.

But, maybe, on days I have to wait . . . I can do my homework first.

It feels wrong. It feels awful. I just want to procrastinate on my phone the whole time, but instead I pull my textbooks from my backpack slowly. I do my math homework and then I finish my history homework too. And when I hear Keisha's boots on the steps and Mom's cheerful call from downstairs, I don't feel nearly as bad as I did when I started.

Maybe this is what Lula meant about being flexible. Maybe things aren't hopeless after all.

Chapter 13

"Is something wrong?" Dani asks me. It's Friday, Dani Time, and we're at the skatepark again.

I shrug, kind of miserable. I felt okay after doing my homework, but then during dinner, Mom and Keisha kept talking with Makayla and barely talked to me at all. I've been in a bad mood since then.

"Come on," Dani coaxes. She rides by me on her skateboard, and attempts a kickflip. She falls flat on her butt, which does make me laugh. "Ouch! Don't laugh! Tell me what's going on."

I sigh. "I don't know, I'm just feeling weird about Makayla."

"Yeah?" Dani raises her eyebrows. Dani likes Makayla, I think, so I hesitate for a while.

"Yeah. On Monday, I kinda yelled at her."

"Whoa. Yelling is not part of the JV Brand." Dani sits next to me, balancing her board on her knee. "What happened?"

"She was trying to get me to like that stupid cat. And she put her on my bed. Right next to me."

Dani winces. "Yikes. Does she know you hate cats?"

"She does now . . ."

Dani shakes her head. "I mean, she shouldn't have done that, so it's her own fault if she got yelled at. Who throws cats at people?"

I look at Dani and I almost feel like crying. At least she's on my side.

"It's been really awkward. Like *really* awkward." I think about our silent ride to school this morning and her rushed goodbye when Dani and I left.

"Uh oh. Did she apologize to you?"

"Well . . . sort of?"

"That doesn't sound too confident."

I sigh. I don't even want to think about it anymore. "It's fine. We're scheduled to hang out tomorrow, so maybe we can make up then."

"Oh! Wait, don't do that. Hang out with me tomorrow."

"Saturday is Family Time—"

"I know! But look at this." Dani pulls out her phone and shows me a flyer for a concert. Wait, is that the Glitter Bombs?! "I can't believe it because Mom's luck is so bad, but she won these tickets on the radio! Just for us!!"

What?! No way! It's like fate. And oh man, I really like the Glitter Bombs. I can't believe they're coming to Lavender Falls! But . . . "I want to, but Saturday is family time."

"Janie, come oooon," Dani groans. "Break schedule just this once! For me! For the band!"

Dani doesn't even like the Glitter Bombs that much, so I know she's doing this for me . . . but I can't. My stomach hurts even worse than it already does when I think about not following the schedule. "Saturday is Family Time. Sorry."

Dani heaves a dramatic sigh. "Okay, fine. I'll record it for you. But if I win any merch, I'm selling it, not giving it to you!"

I push her jokingly and we end up in a play fight. The rest of Dani Time is spent in giggles and very little riding skateboards, which is fine with me. But when I wave at Dani outside her house, and her mom waves back, I really wish I could go to the concert with Dani. I pat my face to dispel the thought. Saturday will be fun! I'll apologize, and Makayla will too, and everything will be back to normal. Everything will be better after tomorrow.

I glance at the clock anxiously. I have everything ready for Family Time, which is always a movie and popcorn at exactly six o'clock. The last couple of times Keisha seemed like she really enjoyed it, and Makayla too, when she wasn't at her dad's. But of course no one is ready. Mom is in the garden, Keisha's in the kitchen, and I haven't even seen Makayla all day! I groan. This family is killing me.

"What's up, Janie?" Keisha asks, poking her head out of the

kitchen. She's dressed really nice for some reason. No work boots anywhere.

"It's almost time for the movie! Have you seen Makayla?"

Keisha frowns. "Makayla's not here. She's with one of her new friends."

I just stare at her. I . . . what? But we said we'd hang out. Our special hang out has been on my schedule for over a week. "But . . . we . . ."

Keisha's frown deepens and I stop myself. I bet Makayla just forgot. And I guess things are kind of awkward . . . But that's okay, we can hang out tomorrow. I mean, I thought it might be nice for all of us to watch a movie together, but if it's just Mom and Keisha, that'll be fun too.

Mom finally comes in from the garden. She's also dressed weirdly nice. She's wearing a pink dress with flowers at the bottom and on the sleeves. I thought she was gardening? "Ah, two of my favorite ladies!" Mom spins around dramatically and when she's facing us again, she's holding three huge daisies.

She gives one to me and one to Keisha, who's doing her gross I'm-in-love look.

"Thanks, Mom." I guess that's what she was doing in the garden. I put my daisy in my pocket, careful not to squish its petals. Keisha is still holding hers like it's a rare treasure.

"I got this one for Makayla when she comes back," Mom says. She skips to the kitchen. "I'll put it in water and then I'll be ready to go!"

"Can you please hurry?" I sigh, glancing at the clock. 6:14 already. "If we don't start the movie soon, we won't be able to play cards after!"

Keisha looks at me, confusion all over her face. "What do you mean?"

What do I mean? I point at the TV. "Saturday is Family Time. We always watch movies together?"

Keisha glares at the kitchen. "Rosie, you said you told her!"

"Oops," Mom says, laughing. She comes back into the living room and kisses Keisha's cheek. "Sorry, Janie, no movie tonight. Keisha and I are going on a date!"

I can't comprehend what she said. She's going on a date . . . ? They're going on a date? But what about Family Time? The movie . . . the popcorn . . .

"I'm so sorry, Janie. I thought you knew," Keisha says. She looks at Mom anxiously. "She'll be here all by herself. Do we have time to call a sitter?"

"A sitter? What? She's twelve!" Mom pats my head, snapping me out of my dumbstruck stupor. "You'll be fine by yourself, right? It's just three hours, tops."

"Oh, umm, yeah. Yeah!" I try my best to sound enthusiastic. "I'll be okay. You have fun!"

Mom kisses my cheek. "Good girl. Be back soon! Come on Keisha, they'll throw out our reservation!"

Keisha still looks anxious. "You're sure, Janie?"

"I'm sure." I smile big, so she won't see any trace of the terrible feeling welling up in my chest. "Have fun! Bring me something back!"

Keisha nods, and hesitates, but follows Mom out the front door. I wave at them from the window, and I don't stop for a while, even after I can't see Keisha's car anymore.

I wander to the couch and turn on the TV, but I'm not watching it. I feel like I'm gonna throw up. I went from four people watching a movie during Family Time to just me. All alone.

But maybe . . . maybe it's not so bad . . . ! I can still watch a movie. I can still pop popcorn for me. I'll even do kettle corn, which I don't normally get to eat because Mom hates it. I try to pump myself up as I pick out a movie (*Jurassic Park*, which Mom wouldn't let me watch last year) and pop one bag of kettle corn. I grab my phone to text Dani, but then I remember she's at the Glitter Bombs concert. I scroll through my phone, feeling a little down. This wouldn't be so bad if Makayla was here, even if we are kind of fighting. Where is she anyway?

I go to Instagram and my thumb freezes over the screen. Piper's posted a picture of her and Kyle, and right in the middle is Makayla. Smiling shyly at the camera. And on Piper's right is Dani, grinning with all her teeth.

They're all at the concert.

Everyone is at the concert without me.

Pressure builds behind my eyes and my phone screen gets blurry. I told Dani I couldn't go because of Family Time, and my whole family left me by myself while they went to have fun. Saturday is Family Time. Saturdays, we watch movies and eat popcorn and play cards. It's been that way for years. And now, suddenly, no one has time for that anymore. No one has time for *me* anymore.

I jump when something moves out of the corner of my eye. Pumpkin hops onto the couch, her ears pricked. I freeze, halfway between sobbing and terror. She's been avoiding me since Monday, which I was thankful for, but now she's just a few feet from me.

"Wh-what is it?" I murmur. My voice trembles with fear and from trying not to cry.

Pumpkin blinks at me and meows. I don't move. She's so close . . . I'm scared, but also too defeated to run away. I sit like a statue and watch Pumpkin ease closer and closer to me, until . . .

She puts her paws on my thigh and climbs into my lap.

I can't breathe. Oh my god, she could scratch me so easily

right now! Or bite me! But . . . she doesn't. She settles on my lap and purrs. I can feel the vibration because she's so close. Oh wow. She's really heavy, but it's not so bad. Some of the pressure behind my eyes fades away.

"Everyone left you too, huh?" Tentatively, I reach out and put one hand on Pumpkin's back. Her fur is so soft and fluffy. She purrs even harder and rubs her face on my palm. As I pet Pumpkin, I feel a little bit better. Maybe there's something to cats after all.

I put my phone down and start the movie, Pumpkin napping on my lap, and try my best to make the best of Family Time (party of two) as I can.

Chapter 14

"Dani Time!" Dani sings after school. I manage to smile as I wheel my bike next to her. We're going to the skatepark again, and I'm glad. It's been a tough few days, and I'm ready to ride my bike for a while and forget everything.

"I was thinking," Dani says, wobbling on her board as we walk toward the skatepark, "do you want to pick what we do today?"

"No way! It's called Dani Time for a reason." I push her playfully, but then have to catch her before she falls on her face.

"Okay! Just checking. We can do Janie Time too sometimes."

I don't say anything, my mind wandering. Lula said something about that too.

We get to the park, but there's yellow tape all over the handrails. Uh oh.

"What?!" Dani puffs up like a bullfrog, which almost makes me laugh. "What's going on?!"

"Sorry, girls," Mr. Parker, the groundskeeper, calls. He's standing in the middle of the taped-off half-pipes and railings, holding a wrench. "The pipes are closed today for repairs."

Dani puffs up even more and I let a giggle escape. I know she's mad, but she's cheering me up. "Sorry, Dani. What else do you want to do?"

Dani mutters under her breath, but doesn't answer. Uh oh, she's actually getting mad . . . I glance around. The skatepark is attached to the town's rec center, so there's all sorts of things to do.

"Oh, what about basketball?"

Dani frowns, but nods. "Okay. I haven't played in forever though."

Me neither, but it does sound fun. In elementary school,

before we lost the apartment, I was on a basketball team. After we got the house, I didn't rejoin. Practice and games didn't fit into the schedule.

We borrow basketballs from inside and soon I'm bouncing the basketball on the dark asphalt. It feels unfamiliar and familiar at the same time. My hands got bigger! But the motion is regular, even, easy.

"Wanna play HORSE?"

"No. I hate horses." Dani shoots a free throw and misses by a mile. I barely contain a laugh as she groans and clutches her hair dramatically. "Stop laughing! How about CAMEL?"

"Deal."

"And," Dani says, hurrying to grab her runaway ball, "if I win, we have to talk about how you're feeling."

"Hmm." I bounce my ball. "Then if I win, it's the other way around." It's almost like my muscles remember exactly what to do. I adjust my feet, aim, and shoot. The ball sails through the air and lands in the hoop with a perfect swish. I grin at Dani with all my teeth. "You sure?"

Dani gapes at me for a second, but then recovers. She puts her hands on her hips, grinning too. "I'm sure! Let's go!"

Dani is so bad at basketball. We play a game of CAMEL and she misses every shot she takes. She gets angrier and angrier as the game goes on, which sends me into fits of giggles.

"This sucks, big-time. I hate basketball!" Dani kicks her ball and it bounces away. She sighs and runs to get it.

"Sorry for ruining Dani Time." I pick up my ball, suddenly uncertain. I had a good time, but this is Dani's time! I should have let her pick. "We can do something else now."

"No! This is fine." Dani gives me a wide grin. "You've cheered up a little."

I bounce my basketball for a while. I do feel better. But I don't know if I'm ready to talk about everything yet. "But you haven't."

Dani shrugs. "I feel fine!"

"No, you're upset too." I pause, then grin at her. "Besides, I won, so we have to talk about your feelings."

"Ugh, I really messed that deal up." Dani is quiet for a

moment, and then bounces her ball too. She doesn't shoot. "Mr. Parker called us 'girls.'"

Ah. I stop bouncing my ball. "But you're not."

"Right." Dani sighs again. "And I know he didn't mean anything by it, but it's just—ugh. I don't know."

I put my ball down and sit on it. Dani does the same. I don't think we'll be playing anymore for a while. "I think I get it. I wouldn't like it if everyone called me a boy."

"Yeah. It's more than that though, you know? I don't just dislike being called a girl, it's wrong. Way wrong."

"But didn't you say you feel more like a girl than a boy sometimes? The sixty-five thing."

Dani is really quiet. She won't look at me, studying her shoes instead. "Well, the scales thing is only kind of true. I read that when you explain being enby to people, that's what you should say."

"Oh." I frown at Dani. Was I thinking the wrong way this whole time? "What's the actual truth?"

"I'm not just more 'girl' than I am 'boy.' Like, gender's not on two lines. It's more like . . . something else entirely."

I think that over. Not a line . . . Not linear . . . Suddenly, my head is full of math models. "It's like a third dimension."

Dani looks up at me, smiling. "Yeah! That's it!"

I nod, mulling that over. Dani's explanation with the scales still just used feminine and masculine. That's still binary—only two options. It's not a question of if Dani is more girl than boy; Dani is saying nonbinary is separate, and doesn't have to rely on those two options to exist. Okay. "Okay, I got it! I mean, I'm pretty sure I do."

"Of course you do. You're the smartest girl I know!"

We high-five, laughing. I wish she'd told me this earlier! I spent a whole year thinking the wrong thing. "So, do you think you'll tell your mom and dad this?"

Dani fidgets. "I don't know. I'm gonna do it soon, but I'm trying to figure out how. And I kind of . . ."

"Kind of what?"

Dani turns to me, her expression serious again. "Remember when I asked you to use *she/they* for my pronouns?" I nod. "Okay, how do you do that?"

I frown, crossing my arms. "Well, when I talk about you with Mom and Keisha, I use *they*."

"You do?" Dani's eyes are shining with hope and gratitude.

"Yeah! You told me to!" I grin at her. "As for *she* . . . That's what I use at school because I didn't want anyone to find out before you told them. But also . . . I guess I still think of you as *she*." I gasp, my hand over my mouth. "But that's wrong, isn't it? Since gender isn't a line."

"Right." Dani takes a shaky breath. "I said I wanted to use *she/they* last year because I was still figuring things out. But I'm sure now. *She/they* isn't for me, because I'm not a girl at all. I think I'm ready for *they/them*."

I meet Dani's eyes. Dani seems so nervous, but so sure too. And happy. I grin.

"Okay. If you're ready, then I'm ready too."

Dani smiles at me and then tackles me into a hug. "I love you, JV! You're the best."

"Yeah, yeah." We laugh and stand up again. Dani picks up their ball, smiling.

"Let's do another game! But I'm gonna win this time. We ended up talking about my drama and not yours!"

"I don't have any drama." I bounce my ball and then shoot. It bounces off the backboard and into the hoop. "Well, maybe a little."

"Yeah?" Dani shoots and makes it in the hoop. They whoop with glee.

"Yeah." I grab my ball and shoot again. I miss this time. "I'm just kinda mad at Piper and Kyle."

"Why?"

"They keep canceling our game on Wednesday. We always play on Wednesdays. Always."

"But you hate D&D, right?"

"Kinda, but that's not the point. That's our time, you know? We haven't hung out in forever. They're always with Makayla." I shoot again, and miss. "And, like, at the concert, Piper just takes Makayla with her. But Makayla was supposed to hang out with *me* on Saturday. Family Time. So not only did she blow me off, neither of them asked me if I wanted to go to the concert with them."

Dani doesn't say anything at first. They shoot and miss too, so we both have to catch our balls before they roll away. "Sounds like Makayla is the main problem."

I don't answer. I get this awful, terrible feeling in my chest when I think about Makayla. At school today, she tried to wave at me, but I didn't wave back because I'm so confused. I just don't understand her, or what's happening with us. I don't understand why she blew me off on Saturday, but at school she acts like she wants to be my friend. And now, at dinner, Mom and Keisha gush to her about making new friends and joining a new club—*my* friends, *my* club—and they barely ask me anything at all. I feel so sick I might throw up right now.

"Dani," I say, shooting my ball. It misses the hoop by a ton and it rolls into the grass. "I think I'm being replaced."

"No way," Dani says. They retrieve my ball and hand it back to me. "I know Makayla's a lot, but you're irreplaceable!" They sing the last part, which makes me laugh a little.

"I'm serious though. She's Piper's friend now, and Mom's daughter. She's taken my whole life."

"Maybe this is like that movie. She's a body snatcher!"

That makes me laugh. I imagine Makayla as an alien, coming to steal my body. I can't really picture it though, because she's always so quiet and shy. "No, it's not like that. I guess she didn't steal anything. Piper and Kyle and Mom are just letting her take them."

Dani seems stricken. "Janie . . ."

I shake my head. "It's fine. I'm fine! I swear, once we can all get back on track with the schedule, it'll all work out."

Dani still seems sad, but smiles. "Yeah. Okay, no more heavy stuff! Come on, one more game of CAMEL before Dani Time is over."

"What happens if I win?"

"You *won't*, but if you do, I'll make buttons for you. For the election!"

I can't help but smile. Dani is trying their best to cheer me up. I know, no matter what Makayla does next, at least Dani will be on my side. They're unstealable.

"Deal."

Chapter 15

For the third Wednesday in a row, I head home instead of staying at school to play D&D with Piper and Kyle. Their excuse this time: *Demon Slayer*. Whatever. I don't like demons or slaying them either. I shake my head to dispel the negative thoughts. The last two Wednesdays I spent at home on my phone, anxiously waiting for dinner and helping Mom with painting, but today I want to try something new. I want to try what Dani and Lula suggested—

Janie Time.

I've been thinking about it all day. Well, really, I've been thinking about a lot of things. Like when I met Piper and Kyle, I just went along with their game because I didn't want them to feel bad about Dani Time. I don't like D&D, but I didn't say anything. I just endured it. And then when I played basketball with Dani, I had fun. I forgot that I'm good at basketball! I want to play again, but the handrails at the skatepark will be fixed soon. I can't help but feel disappointed. I also can't help but feel like I'm on the edge of discovering something big about myself, and Janie Time will get me there.

When I get home, Mom is in her studio. Pumpkin charges toward me from the kitchen, yowling. I freeze in fear, but cautiously relax when she rubs her face against my legs. Since our lonely Saturday, I've decided Pumpkin is sort of okay. Scary, and I don't trust her fully, but I can tolerate her being friendly sometimes.

"Okay, Pumpkin," I say out loud. Her ears prick and she looks up at me. "What should I do first?" I didn't really plan anything for Janie Time; I just wanted to try whatever came to mind. But maybe I should have thought about something . . .

Pumpkin meows loudly, startling me out of my thoughts. She trots into the kitchen and then back to me, yowling at the top of her lungs.

"Okay! Okay, hold on." I follow her to the kitchen and open the cabinet for her cat food. I guess step one of Janie Time is feeding a cat that doesn't belong to me.

I grab a bag of treats and I swear Pumpkin's eyes grow twice as big. She circles me, yelling as loud as possible. How does Makayla stand this?

"Shh, shh. Here." I drop one treat and Pumpkin attacks it, fluffy tail twitching. She looks up at me for another, her green eyes round. Aww . . . for a second, she's almost cute. Almost.

"Okay, one more." I start to drop another treat, but I pause. Janie Time is all about doing something unplanned, right? So maybe I could . . . I put the treat in my palm, my heart hammering against my ribs. I hold my breath, bend at the waist, and extend my hand to Pumpkin. "Oh god. Please don't bite me, I'm begging—"

Pumpkin takes the treat from my hand, her whiskers tickling

my palm. She licks my hand too, her tongue like sandpaper against my skin.

"Oh wow." My voice is hushed as Pumpkin crunches happily on her treat. She didn't bite me . . . ! I can't believe it! She was actually nice! I watch Pumpkin clean her whiskers in awe.

I shake my head to clear it. I still can't trust cats, but this feels like a tiny step forward! Still, I can't spend all of Janie Time playing with Pumpkin. I need to do something else.

Pumpkin follows me around as I try different things. I pick up a book, but I don't feel like reading. Same with a magazine, and then the sketch pad Mom gave me for Christmas. I'm not feeling it. I cross my arms, staring outside at Mom painting in her studio. I wish I had something I liked as much as she likes painting. She's always humming and smiling when she paints, even when she's stuck, even when she messes up and has to start over. I want to be that happy too.

Pumpkin headbutts my leg, startling me. She purrs and rubs her face against me, then rolls onto her back. She *is* pretty cute . . . but wait!

"Nice try," I say, stepping around her. "But Makayla told me your belly is a trap. No, thanks." I can't be sure Makayla isn't stretching the truth, like she does about school, but it's too risky to try.

I climb the stairs and Pumpkin hurries after me. I don't even try to keep her out of my room this time. I think I made a mistake with the treats . . . I'll never get rid of her now. But I think that's okay. As long as she's not biting or scratching me, she can hang out in my room.

Pumpkin makes a beeline for my dirty clothes pile, and I sit at my desk. It's already been thirty minutes, but I haven't done anything yet! Janie Time is a waste of time so far. I pull out my phone and start to touch Instagram, but . . . I really don't want to see Piper and Kyle hanging out without me. I touch YouTube instead, something I've only used for math homework lately. At first, I scroll through my recommendations, which is just school stuff, but then I see it: an ad for *Resident Evil*. Dani and I are gonna play as soon as the election is over, which is soon, thank goodness. But . . . when can we play? During Dani Time? But they'll want to skateboard too sometimes, surely? When I start a game, I have to finish it as soon as possible or I'll be dreaming about it at all times.

Well . . . I used to do that. I used to play a lot of games. I get up from my desk and go to my bookshelf, where my Switch sits. It's covered with a thick layer of dust. How long has it been since I played? In the summer, sometime? Games aren't in the schedule.

I pick up my Switch, but it's dead. It'll take forever to charge now. I glance at my phone again. I don't want to watch a play-through of *Resident Evil* without Dani, but maybe I could watch another game?

I pick one at random—*Cuphead*? The guy who's playing has a squeaky voice and is hilarious. He keeps dying, over and over! I laugh along with him, and I watch him finally beat the first boss. And I keep watching as he beats the second and third boss. And when my desk chair gets too hard, I sit on the floor next to Pumpkin, who curls up beside my thigh and purrs herself to sleep.

"Janie?" I look up and pause my video. Mom's peeking into my room. She smiles at me. "What're you doing?"

"Umm." I glance at my paused phone, and Pumpkin curled up beside me. "Just . . . hanging out."

"Oh yeah? I heard you laughing up here. Came to see what all the fun was about!" Mom frowns when she sees Pumpkin. "Oh, sorry, Janie. Did I leave the door open again?"

"No." I almost want to pet Pumpkin, but I don't. "It's okay, this time."

"Well, if you're sure. Anyway, it's dinnertime."

Really?! I check my phone and I'm shocked—it's 5:45. I watched videos for a whole hour and a half. Whoa.

"Keisha texted me and said she has a work party, so she won't be joining us for dinner," Mom continues. "And Makayla is at her friend's house. It's just you and me tonight!"

Oh. So we can be on time for dinner . . . ! For once! My chest fills with giddy glee. "Can I help you cook this time?"

"Girl, no! We are getting takeout!" Mom laughs and I smile,

even though I'm a little disappointed. I love helping Mom cook. "Get ready and meet me downstairs, okay? You can pick where we go."

"Okay. Be there in a minute."

Mom leaves, but I don't get up from the floor right away. I need to think.

Janie Time was fun. I had *fun* today. I fed Pumpkin a treat and watched videos and even just walking around and opening books and magazines was relaxing. But now I'm feeling uneasy. If Piper and Kyle hadn't decided to ditch me, I wouldn't have had this time at all. Because fun is not on the schedule.

My stomach is killing me. I wrap my arms around myself, the thought killing me too. I haven't had so much fun in forever. I want to play my Switch again. I want to play *Resident Evil* with Dani. I want to play basketball. I want to be happy, like Mom is with her paintings. And to do that, I think I have to change the schedule.

No. No, I can't do that. Because today, for the first time in weeks, we're having dinner on time. When it's just me and

Mom, we can do it. We can be on schedule and everything will work out. I just have to find a way to get everyone to work it out too.

Pumpkin puts her head on my knee, her eyes closed, and I tentatively touch my thumb to her head. She purrs as I stroke her forehead. My stomach hurts worse now, and I can't tell if it's from the thought of changing the schedule or the thought of not having time to pet Pumpkin's sleepy, dumb head like this again.

"I gotta go, Pumpkin." I ease her head off my knee, carefully so I don't wake her. She doesn't wake up; instead, she makes a grumbly sound in her throat and rolls over to her back. "I'm not falling for that." Still, I can't stop smiling.

I get dressed and go downstairs to meet Mom. She smiles at me. "Ready to go?"

"Yep." We go to the car, and I climb into the front seat, like I used to when it was just us two. Back when things were a lot simpler.

Mom cranks up the car. She pauses before pulling out of the driveway. "Janie? Did you have fun today?"

I think back on my day, on my phone with 15 percent battery, on the cat fur on my pants, on my thumbs itching to play a new game. And the knowledge I have to put all that away so I can get this family back on track.

"Yeah." I can't keep the slight sadness out of my voice. "I did."

Chapter 16

Today is election day!

After the final school bell, I head to Sunshine Club. No one else was interested in running, not even Dani, so I'm not worried. But still, it's exciting! One vote away from being Sunshine Club president. I'll have a lot of new responsibilities . . . and no extra free time to take care of them. I chew on my bottom lip, suddenly nervous.

I walk into the clubroom and Dani is chatting with Kyle, while Makayla and Piper are talking on the other side of the room. Things are still kind of awkward with Makayla, even after we talked. I should really try and smooth things over, like I promised Lula I would . . . and now I have time, right before—

"Janie!" Mrs. Clarity calls, snapping my attention to her. She motions for me to come closer. "Come here, come here! You're the last one to vote!"

Oh man, I'm late! I jog to her side, and she gives me a pen and a ripped-up piece of notebook paper. Not fancy, but it works. I write my name on the piece of paper, fold it up, and drop it into a red plastic cup.

Mrs. Clarity beams at me. "Okay, I'll tally the votes! This is so exciting!"

I laugh and nod. I'm glad Mrs. Clarity is just as excited as I am.

I hover between Makayla and Dani, unsure. I should talk to Makayla. I really should. But Mrs. Clarity is tallying the votes as we speak, and she'll be done soon. I should sit down and talk with Makayla at home. Maybe during dinner! That way I won't be off schedule. I nod to myself and join Dani and Kyle instead.

Dani is in the middle of a story about their math teacher, and how he got so mad at the class today, he made everyone stand at the board and do subtraction problems.

"Have you ever subtracted three from a thousand like a hundred times?! Horrible," Dani groans.

"But weren't you the one who got everyone in trouble?" I tease. They told me this story at lunch.

Dani puffs up their chest in indignation. "Yes, I was talking, but I *had* to educate Kenny about Steph Curry. Can you believe he said LeBron is better?"

"LeBron is better," Kyle says, grinning.

"What?!" Dani looks like they're gonna faint. "My own friend betrays me?!"

"Janie agrees," Kyle says, meeting my eyes. His are full of barely contained laughter. I grin back, but hold my hands up.

"I plead the fifth."

"This is outrageous! Lose my number, you two. Never talk to me again."

Kyle and I are laughing when Piper's voice interrupts us.

"Kyle! Come here!"

Kyle looks over and a troubled expression crosses his face. For some reason, he looks at me, his gray eyes kind of sad. "See you around, Janie."

"Oh, uh, okay." I watch him, confused, as he joins Makayla and Piper's group. I look at Dani and they seem confused too.

"That was weird to you, right?"

"Yeah." I watch Kyle for a second, who is talking urgently with Piper, almost like they're arguing. Makayla seems confused too; she's standing by herself now, watching them argue in whispers. "Why'd he look so sad?"

"I don't know," Dani says, their eyebrows pinched together, "but I have a bad feeling about this."

I don't get to answer because Mrs. Clarity stands at the front of the room. We all crowd around as she beams at us.

"Thank you, everyone, for voting! This is such an exciting time. A new club, candidates battling it out, the thrill of democracy . . ."

"Just tell us who won!" Alice calls and everyone laughs.

Mrs. Clarity waits until we're done before clearing her throat. "Well, that's a tricky question, because it's a tie!"

I blink at her, stunned into silence. A . . . a tie? A tie?! What?! I thought I was the only one running?

Dani looks at me, mouth open. "But how? Janie was the only candidate."

"Yep, but we had five write-in votes for another member!"

But who? I look around the room, confused. Me, Dani, Makayla, and Alice and her best friend are shocked, but no one else seems confused. In fact, Piper is staring right at me, a smirk on her face.

Mrs. Clarity turns to Piper's group, smiling. "Congratulations, Makayla!"

Makayla? Makayla?! She just joined three weeks ago! She never said she wanted to be president!

"But I—" Makayla starts, wringing her shirt anxiously, but Piper interrupts her.

"Congratulations! We'll have a president who deserves it!"

Deserves it? What?! Dani and I built this club. We built it from scratch. How can Makayla deserve to be president over me? Suddenly, I'm hot all over. My head swims with disorienting static, and my chest is tight. How is this happening? What *is* happening?

"You better explain what's going on, Piper." Dani stands next to me, their arms crossed. Some of the static leaves my head. Dani's on my side. They're here. I almost want to grab their hand, so I can make sure this is all real.

Piper folds her arms too. "I just think the president of Sunshine Club should be a good person. One who doesn't bully her sister."

Another round of shock hits me. "What?! I don't bully anyone!"

"Then how come you've been ignoring Makayla for a week?" Piper's looking at me like she has some kind of trump card, but I'm bewildered. We talked this morning on the way to school. It was short and awkward, but we did talk. This is coming out of nowhere. I don't understand.

"We fought about Pumpkin, but we're cool now?" I told Makayla to forget it; I know I did.

"That's not what Makayla said."

I look at Makayla, stunned. "Makayla? Say something. Come on."

Makayla's shrunk away from the group, wringing her shirt into knots. She looks really overwhelmed, like she's feeling her chest constrict. Just like mine. Makayla meets my eyes . . . and then looks down at her feet and doesn't say a word.

"Really not cool of you to bully her, Janie," one of the upperclassmen says.

"Yeah," Piper says, her eyes locked on me. "Not cool."

My ears are ringing. Makayla knows I don't bully her. We haven't talked, but I've been really nice to her. If anything, she's been bullying *me*—she blew me off to hang with Piper, she won't talk to me on the bus rides to the nursing home, she freaking threw Pumpkin on my bed! With a jolt of horror, I realize she's doing what she does at the table with Mom and Keisha—she's stretching the truth. No, she's *lying*. She's taking another thing from me, and my friends are just going to let her.

"Umm, girls?" Mrs. Clarity steps between us, her hands out like she's going to stop a fistfight. "It's a tie, remember? We'll have a runoff election in two weeks. Everyone just be calm, okay?"

"Okay," I say, glaring at the people I thought were my friends. Kyle looks sorry, but he's on Piper's side of the room, not with me and Dani. He's not defending me either. And Makayla is still looking away, like this whole thing isn't her fault.

"We'll settle this in two weeks, everyone. For now, it's time to go to the park," Mrs. Clarity says. "Trash won't pick up itself!"

"Sure thing, Mrs. Clarity!" Dani says. "But hang on one second. Janie and I forgot something." Dani grabs my hand and pulls me out of the room. I start shaking as soon as I'm out of there. I can't believe it. I can't believe this.

"You okay?" Dani says, their voice low.

I blink back tears and take a deep breath. "I'm okay." Then I let out a short, strangled laugh. It's hitting me now—Piper and Kyle aren't my friends anymore. They can't be, not after what they did. They couldn't have voted for me. "At least I don't have to play D&D anymore."

"A win as far as I'm concerned." Dani squeezes my hand, really tight. "You sure you want to go back? We can skip today."

"No, let's go back." I can't let them win. I don't understand why they did this, but I have to win the runoff now. I can't miss any more club activities for two weeks. And I have to somehow convince everyone Makayla was lying. All while sticking to my schedule. Uncomfortable heat fills my face and my stomach groans in pain.

Dani nods and squeezes my hand again. "You're right. Let's go. And JV? I believe you. I'm always on your side. Promise."

I smile at Dani, hiding the hurt in my chest. "Thanks, Dani. Let's go to the park. The ducks don't care if we're sad."

Dani laughs and we go back into the clubroom. It's the same

as it always is, but I feel totally different now. The energy is tense and depressing, and Piper, Kyle, and three of the upperclassmen just ignore me. But that's fine. I know I deserve to be president. I just have to convince everyone else.

Chapter 17

We're forty minutes late for dinner, and I'm in a real bad mood.

Mom was on time picking us up from Sunshine Club, but I couldn't be happy about it because of how the election went. I couldn't even look at Makayla on the drive home, while Mom chattered about her new painting. And of course Keisha was still at work, so I tried to do my homework before dinner, like I did before. But I couldn't do that either. I'm just so angry, I can't focus. I can't figure out why Makayla would do this. I can't figure out what I did to make her hate me.

So now my stomach is rolling with panic, my head hurts, *and* I'm starving. This has to be the worst day I've had in a long time.

"Sorry, sorry, we're almost ready!" Mom calls from the kitchen. I'm sitting at my usual chair, but Makayla is on the opposite side of me, as far away as possible. Which is good, but now I keep looking up and catching her eye. Ugh.

Keisha carries a steaming pot into the dining room and my mood lifts a little. We're having spaghetti! The day can't be too bad if spaghetti is involved. Keisha smiles at me as she sits next to Makayla. "Look who's excited!"

"It's my favorite," I admit, already reaching for the pot.

"She knows!" Mom comes into the dining room carrying a basket of garlic bread. She puts it in the middle of the table and kisses Keisha, smiling too. "I told her it was your favorite. You seemed kind of down today, so I thought it might cheer you up."

I can't hold back a smile. I'm glad Mom noticed. Maybe today is salvageable.

We all get busy eating, and for a second, I'm too distracted by how good this spaghetti is to think about anything else. Did Mom use a new kind of sauce? Or new meat? This is so good!

"So, how was school?" Keisha asks, and my good mood is immediately soured. She's looking at Makayla, and I look at Makayla too. She winces when she meets my eyes.

"It was good," she mumbles, eating another forkful of spaghetti.

Good?! Well, maybe it was good for her. Maybe she wanted to see my friends betray me. I'm getting that weird sharp feeling again, just under my ribs.

"Are you sure?" Keisha frowns and puts down her fork. "You don't sound like it was good."

Makayla doesn't say anything for a second, but then looks up at Keisha and smiles. "It was fine, Mom. I promise."

Wow. The sharp feeling increases, digging into my bones.

"Well, I had a pretty bad day."

There's silence at the table. I blink in surprise—I didn't mean to say that out loud!

"What happened?" Mom asks me. She's frowning now too.

I fidget, unsure how to get out of this one. I don't want to blame Makayla, even if I'm mad at her. It'll seem like I'm whining about the election, and that's not the problem at all. I take a deep breath. "Well, Makayla and I tied for Sunshine Club president."

"Oh!" Mom and Keisha look at each other for a second, smiling. "That's so cool! I'm so glad, Makayla, you really seem to like it there. So you'll both be president?"

I didn't even think about that, actually. We *could* share. But I look at Makayla and think about how she lied and ruined my friendship with Piper and Kyle, and that sharp feeling feels like it'll cut me in two.

"No," I say, staring right at Makayla, "there'll be a runoff. And I want to win."

Makayla looks close to tears. That sharp feeling disappears and it's replaced by guilt. I shouldn't be doing this. Even if she hurt me first, I shouldn't hurt her too. I look back at Mom and Keisha, who seem really uncomfortable now, and smile.

"But it'll be a fun competition!" I hurry to clarify. "We can make flyers and stuff."

"Oh," Mom says. She looks relieved. "Yeah, it'll be fun! Have you thought about your strategy? Any new ideas for the club?"

I listen to Makayla stumble through her ideas while I eat my spaghetti. What is wrong with me? Ever since Makayla came to live with us, things have changed. I've changed. I can't believe I said all those things out loud. I really need to think about what to do. Or maybe I can just avoid Makayla until after the election. Focus on that first, and then everything else will fall into place.

I chant that to myself as I go upstairs to do my homework after dinner. Pumpkin, of course, is in my room. She jumps to her feet when I come in and rubs against my ankles. I sigh and just let her. I can't fight it anymore. She likes me, for some reason, so as long as she doesn't scratch me, I guess it's okay if she hangs out in here.

I sit at my desk and Pumpkin busies herself with batting around my untied shoestring. I have so much homework today, but I also need to find some time for the election. I need to actually campaign this time. Make flyers, maybe buttons? More cookies? But really, the big problem is . . . how do I convince everyone that Makayla was lying about me?

I hear the creak of the stairs and stiffen when someone pushes open my door. I turn around, reluctantly, and it's who I feared: Makayla.

She's fidgeting a lot and not looking at me. "Umm, I know you don't like Pumpkin in your room. So I came to get her."

"Okay."

But neither of us moves. Pumpkin is still playing around under my chair, so I need to move so Makayla can pick her up. But I don't want to move. I don't feel like always being the one to move so Makayla can take up more and more of my space.

"Umm." Makayla takes a shaky, nervous breath. She's still not looking up. "I'm sorry about how things went today. I really am."

I turn back to my desk, conflicted. I'm glad she apologized. She *did* look surprised when Mrs. Clarity announced the results.

I bet this was Piper's plan, not hers. But she still lied to Piper in the first place, and I'm not ready to forgive her for that.

"Yeah. Me too."

From the corner of my eye, I see Makayla's face fall. I sigh.

"You can leave Pumpkin in here. It's okay."

"But aren't you scared of . . ." Makayla trails off, then backs out of my room. "Never mind. I'll just—I'll just go. I'll see you tomorrow, Janie."

"Yeah."

I don't say anything as she leaves. And I feel so terrible—about the runoff, about her lying, about how things got so bad that we can't even talk to each other—that I spend twice as long as usual finishing my homework. When I shower and finally climb into bed, I know it's going to take me forever to fall asleep.

Chapter 18

I'm lying facedown on my bed, Pumpkin perched on my back, when I hear my door open. I don't move though. I'm too tired to move. Pumpkin followed me in here after school and I didn't even have the energy to kick her off my bed.

"Hmm," Mom says. "Looks like we're having a rough day."

"Kinda."

I hear Mom's footsteps approach and then Pumpkin's soothing weight is lifted from my back. I hear her hiss at Mom, which makes me look up. But it's okay; Mom places her on the floor and Pumpkin flounces out of my room, tail held high.

Mom smiles at me. "Rescued you from the big bad lion. You're welcome."

"You mean the big fluffy basketball." I sit up and sit on the edge of my bed, feeling sluggish. It's Wednesday again, and I thought I wouldn't be upset about D&D being over, but it kind of hurts. It hurts enough that I don't feel like doing homework or thinking about the election or even doing Janie Time like I did last week. I just want to lie on my bed and sleep. And honestly, having Pumpkin purring on my back helped. I was almost asleep.

Mom sits next to me and pulls me into a one-armed hug. I lean against her, a little comforted. "You've been feeling down lately, huh?"

I snuggle closer to Mom, tears pricking my eyes. She noticed. I'm really, really glad she noticed. "Yeah."

Mom nods and hugs me tighter. "Is it dinner? I know how upset you get when we're not on time."

Not really, but that is a problem . . .

"How about this," Mom continues. "What if we start having dinner at seven instead of six? I'll pack you an extra snack to eat after school so you're not so hungry, and you can put something else in from six to seven. What do you think?"

My stomach groans in pain and I hug my middle. No. No, I don't want to eat at seven—I want to eat at six, like we've done for years, like we've done for forever. Why do I always have to change, when what we were doing worked fine?

"No?" Mom asks when I'm silent.

"I want to try and stick to the original schedule," I mumble. I know I should consider changing dinnertime to seven, but I don't feel good. For once, I want something to go my way.

"Okay." Mom strokes my hair, her hands gentle. "Then what's going on? What can I do to help?"

I sigh. I might as well be honest. "I'm supposed to play D&D with Piper and Kyle on Wednesdays. But I'm not."

"Did something happen?"

I sniffle before answering. "Yeah. We're not friends anymore."

Mom sucks in a breath and hugs me closer. "I'm sorry, Janie. Middle school is always a hard time with friends. Lots of moving and changing. It's normal."

I don't think what Makayla is doing is normal. "Maybe. But they're not my friends anymore because of Makayla."

"What do you mean?"

"I mean she's . . ." I trail off, struggling. I still don't want to tell on her, even now.

"You mean they voted for her over you?" Mom asks.

"Yeah! They did. They're my friends. They're supposed to be on my side."

Mom nods, rubbing my arm with one thumb. "Yes, but they're Makayla's friends too. Maybe don't be so hard on them. It's a hard choice to make."

I pull away from Mom, incredulous. "Mom, she didn't even *want* to be president. They voted for her just so I wouldn't get it."

Mom frowns. "But Makayla loves Sunshine Club. She told me that she really enjoys her time there."

Okay? So what? She never even mentioned wanting to run for president. She knew I wanted this. She knew how much it meant to me. She even offered to help me with the election! I just don't get it.

"I know this is hard, Janie. Getting a new sister is hard. But let's try to be kind, okay? Makayla is still getting her feet on the ground in a new school. We want to be supportive."

I *was* supportive. And then she betrayed me. This just isn't fair. "Mom, I really feel like I'm being replaced."

"What? No! Of course not." Mom gives me a hug, but it doesn't make me feel any better. "No one is replacing you. This is just a weird transition time. It'll get better. You'll see."

I don't say anything. She's not listening to me. She never does. "Okay, Mom."

Mom kisses the top of my head. "I'll leave you be, but let me know if you want to talk about Piper and Kyle. Maybe we can brainstorm on how to make up with them."

"Okay." But there's no point in talking with Mom. She won't listen to me. She just takes Makayla's side all the time, and that's Piper and Kyle's side too.

Mom leaves, and I lie back down on my bed. Maybe for Janie Time I can just take a nap. I still have dinner and homework and election planning to get through, but for now everything is quiet in my room. In the quiet, alone, it feels like the only place I can have some peace.

I hug Lula on Thursday as soon as I see her. She hugs me back and kisses the top of my head.

"Things not going so well, huh?"

Not at all. Not even a little. It's been over a week and the runoff is really soon. But I feel like I haven't made any progress. Everyone except for Dani and Alice just ignores me. Makayla and I haven't talked in forever. I even brought cookies again, but only Dani and I ate them. Everything sucks.

But I just smile and sit down after our hug. "It's okay. More important: Did you hear from your daughter yet?"

Lula rolls her eyes. "Always moving so fast."

"But did you?"

Lula won't look at me. She just sets up the checkerboard, really slowly. "Have you made up with Makayla yet? You didn't walk in together."

I hesitate, watching Lula place checkers carefully on our

board. She sounds a little off. Did something happen? "Umm . . .
not really. But can we talk about Margaret? Did she answer your
letter?" I gasp, realizing what day it is. "The karaoke night! That
was yesterday, right? How'd it go?"

Lula stops putting checkers on the board. She still won't
look at me. "She came to the karaoke night."

"Ah, Lula! That's so exciting!"

But Lula doesn't look excited. She just keeps staring at the
table. "Where were you, Janie? The other club members came. I
was looking for you."

What? But I'm sure I told her I couldn't come. "Lula, it
wasn't on the schedule, so I—"

"Bah, forget it." Lula nudges the board toward me. "You go
first."

I do, but I'm full of unease. Something's wrong. Something
happened. "Lula, did you make up with Margaret?"

Lula finally looks up at me. Her eyes are sad. "Did you make
up with Makayla? Same answer."

"Oh no. I'm so sorry, Lula."

"It's okay. It was a long shot. She is so stubborn, just like you." Lula laughs to herself as she moves one of her checkers. "Just like me."

"Maybe we can write another letter, or call her—"

"No, it's okay. It's too late." Lula sighs. "We tried. I just wish you'd have been there last night. I don't like any of those other kids. And they all sing so bad."

Lula laughs, but I don't. Lula wanted me to be here and I let her down. I was just moping yesterday. I could have come. I should have come. The schedule is important for me and Mom, really important, but I never thought it would hurt Lula. I play checkers with Lula, but I feel bad for the rest of the hour. We talk, like normal, except now her voice is unsteady and her expression pinched with sadness. I want to say something, do something, but Lula just hugs me tight when it's time to go and shuffles to her room. Away from me.

Something has to change. I just wish I knew what to do.

Chapter 19

When I get home from Sunshine Club, I practically run upstairs to avoid Makayla. I may have to skip dinner. She looks like she really wants to talk to me, and I really, really don't want to talk back.

Pumpkin's on my bed. Just sitting there, at the foot of my bed, like she belongs there. Wow. She meows when she sees me, but doesn't move.

"Hi, Pumpkin. Don't scratch me, okay? I'm just gonna . . ." I climb onto my bed, far away from her. I settle carefully on one side, but Pumpkin meows again and flops down next to me. She starts purring as I tentatively pet her head.

"What kind of cat are you?" I pet her, bemused. "You must be a dog-cat hybrid. You're too nice."

Pumpkin just purrs, kneading her paws on my comforter. At least she's not scratching me. I'll take it.

I pull out my phone and I'm about to sneak-watch another episode of the *Cuphead* playthrough when my phone jerks itself out of my hands. What on earth . . . ? It's vibrating against my knee—oh! Someone's calling me. Wow. I don't think that's ever happened.

I pick up my phone and glance at the screen. It's Dani. Dani has never called me, not an unplanned voice call anyway. I answer, a little scared.

"Hello?"

"H-hey, JV." Dani's voice is so soft I can barely hear them. "Sorry to bother you."

"You're not bothering me." I hesitate. Something's wrong. Dani sounds like they're trying not to cry. "What's up?"

Dani takes a shaky breath. "I know it's not Dani Time," they say, "and I know it's not on your schedule, but could you come over?"

"Right now?" I can't go to Dani's; it's Thursday, and we're about to eat dinner, on time for once, and—

"You don't have to." Dani's voice cracks, right at the end.

I freeze. They're crying.

I glance at my open planner on my desk. It's not Dani Time. It's almost dinnertime, and Keisha is here so we might actually be close to on time. But Dani's crying. They need me.

This isn't on the schedule. But I'm realizing the schedule doesn't have a lot of things on it. Fun, for starters. Or surprise Glitter Bombs concerts. Or karaoke nights when your friend needs your support to talk to her daughter.

Or when your best friend is crying on a Thursday and they need you.

I said something has to change. I think this is it.

I take a deep breath. "I'm on my way."

"R-really?"

"Really." I jump off my bed and pull on my shoes. "I'll be there in just a second, okay?"

"Okay." Dani's voice is soft again. "Thanks, Janie."

160

"No problem. Be there soon!"

I hang up and put my phone in my pocket. I don't feel so good. My heart beats double time and my stomach feels like someone is wringing it out like a dishrag. But I take a shaky, deep breath and wipe my sweaty palms on my shorts. I'm breaking schedule, *on purpose*, but this is important. Dani hardly ever cries, and they know how much the schedule means to me. This has to be an emergency. And I already missed something important to Lula because of the schedule . . . Not again. So, even though I feel like I'm going to throw up, I push through and run downstairs.

Mom and Keisha are in the kitchen. No Makayla, thank goodness. I glance at the window—it's getting dark. I hope they let me go . . .

"Mom, can I go to Dani's house?"

Mom turns around, her eyes huge. "What? It's almost dinnertime."

"I'll eat dinner there." I take a deep breath. "Please? Can I go?"

Mom and Keisha look at each other and I wait, my heart in my throat.

"Well, I mean . . ." Mom hesitates. "I guess so. Text me when you get there, okay?"

"Okay! Thanks, Mom!"

"Wait, Janie," Keisha says. "I can drive you."

"No, thanks." I make sure my voice sounds firm. Keisha takes *forever* to get ready. I need to get to Dani's ASAP. "I'll take my bike. Bye!"

I run out the door before Mom can change her mind. My bike is by the garage, so I scramble onto it and ride as fast as I can to Dani's house.

It only takes seven minutes to walk from my house to Dani's, but on my bike I make it in four. I'm gasping for breath when I knock on their door.

Dani's mom answers. Her eyes widen in surprise. "Oh, Janie! What're you doing here?"

"Umm . . ." I think up a lie as fast as I can. "Dani and I are doing a project for school. They wanted me to come over so we can finish it."

Dani's mom frowns, but steps back so I can come in.

"Okay . . . Dani's in their room. Let me know if you need anything!"

Except, Dani's mom doesn't say "their." I don't think that's a good sign. I wave and go to Dani's room, which is on the first floor. They have their door closed, so I knock.

"Dani? Can I come in?"

"Janie?" I hear muffled movement, and then their door opens. Dani's eyes are red and raw, and their cheeks are flushed. Pain surges through my chest. They *were* crying. I knew it.

Dani gives me a wobbly smile. "JV breaking the schedule. I never thought I'd see the day."

"I'm always full of surprises!"

"I think it's just the one surprise." Dani laughs a little and opens their door wide. "Come in."

Dani's room is a big mess. I'm not kidding. There are clothes everywhere, and toys and games and paper litter the floor. They swear they can find everything when they need it, but there's just no way. I pick through the clutter to sit on their bed. Their desk chair is currently holding a big, yellow plush seahorse.

Dani closes the door and sits next to me, closer than they normally would. We just sit together for a minute, listening to their parents' muffled voices in the kitchen. My heart rate slows and my palms are dry. I was anxious before, but I'm calm now. This is where I need to be, schedule or not.

Dani takes a breath. "I'm sorry, Janie. I know you hate getting off your schedule."

"It's okay. It's been kinda rough anyway. And I don't have to eat dinner with Makayla so that's great."

"I don't think you'll get to eat dinner here either." Dani sighs heavily. "I can't go out there right now."

I sit in silence for a few seconds. I bump Dani's knee with mine. "What happened?"

"I got in a fight with Dad." Tears well up in Dani's eyes. "I tried . . . I tried telling him I'm enby. And I wanted him to use *they/them* pronouns."

My stomach sinks to my toes. I thought so. "What'd he say?"

"He kept saying I was just confused, and this is a phase. But it's not a phase! I know how I feel." Anxiety crosses Dani's face.

"Now I do feel confused though. I feel awful. Like I'm gonna throw up."

I take a moment to think. Dani seemed so happy when we played basketball, and when they asked me to use their pronouns. It's not fair that their mom and dad made them cry. They said they were sure, and I hate that their parents made them doubt that.

"I don't think you're confused. Not about being enby."

"Yeah?"

"Yeah. I think you're confused about why your dad didn't accept what you said. Like, how hard is it to just listen to your kid when they talk?" I think about Mom not listening to me about Pumpkin (and Makayla, and the schedule), and wince. "Sometimes parents suck. But friends don't. I believe you, Dani. You're enby and a great skater and a lousy singer and my best friend. If you need me, I'm here. Any time is Dani Time."

Dani stares at me for a long moment, and then their eyes fill with tears. "You're so freaking cool, JV."

A laugh bubbles out of me, so loud and sudden it scares me a little. But then Dani starts laughing and the tense, heartbroken bubble is broken. They give me a huge hug and everything is almost back to normal.

I end up staying for hours. We do our homework and Dani's mom brings us dinner. At nine o'clock, Dani's mom tells me that Mom and Keisha are coming to pick me up, so I gather all my stuff.

"Hey, JV."

I turn around and Dani's watching me with a serious expression. "Yeah?"

"Thanks for coming over. I thought . . . I felt so bad."

"But you feel better now?"

"Yeah. A lot better." Dani smiles at me. "I meant what I said, JV. You're really cool. And if you ever want to plot revenge against Makayla or come up with an election speech, let me know."

I smile back as Mom calls my name. "Thanks. Maybe at the next Dani Time."

"I thought you said that was anytime!"

We laugh and go to the living room together. Mom and

Keisha are close to the door, where they're chatting with Dani's mom.

"Thanks for taking care of our studious girl!" Mom tells Dani's mom, pulling me into a one-armed hug.

"No problem at all! I wish she'd rub off on our not-so-studious girl," Dani's mom laughs. Dani winces at the word *girl*, but doesn't say anything.

That strange, unfamiliar heat surges up and I stand straighter. "Dani's not a girl," I interrupt. Everyone gets really quiet, and even though nervous heat creeps up my neck, I keep going. "They're nonbinary and you should respect that."

No one says anything for a long second, and then Mom bursts into laughter. "Atta girl, Janie! You tell 'em."

Dani looks from me to Mom with wonder. They smile at me and I smile back.

Anxiety crosses Dani's mom's face and she leans closer to Mom. "Rosie, can I borrow you for a second?"

"Sure," Mom says. She smiles at me. "Will you wait in the car with Keisha?"

I nod, and give Dani a hug. They hug me super tight, and right before they let go, they say, "Thanks, JV."

"You're welcome," I whisper back. I wave at Dani, and Keisha and I leave Dani's house together.

Keisha puts my bike in the trunk and then sits in the passenger seat, which means I'm in the back. I'm relieved Makayla's not here. Keisha looks back at me as I buckle my seat belt. "I didn't know your friend is nonbinary."

"Yeah. They are."

Keisha nods. She seems thoughtful. "Coming out gone bad?"

Whoa, how'd she know? Although, I guess she had to come out to her parents too. "Yeah. They don't believe Dani. But I do."

Keisha smiles at me. "I'm glad Dani has a good friend in you. Coming out is hard, especially if the people you love aren't accepting. But I think they'll be fine."

"You think so?"

Keisha nods at Mom and Dani's mom saying goodbye on Dani's porch. "Their mom is trying. She could have gotten mad at you for what you said, but she didn't. She knows what you said was right." Keisha smiles at me. "They'll come around. And if not, we'll just have to adopt Dani, huh?"

I smile back as Mom opens the driver's-side door. "Whew, what a night! Janie, remind me to raise your allowance."

"I don't get an allowance."

"Then you do now!" Mom laughs, but then gets serious a second later. She meets my eyes in the rearview mirror. "Janie, if you ever want to come out to us, know that we're safe."

"Umm, okay." I don't have anything to come out about, but that's really nice that she said that.

"About anything at all," Keisha adds. "Not just gender, or who you like, you know?"

I think uneasily about Makayla. "Umm, okay."

"And about any changes too," Mom says. "There's a time in every kid's life when certain body changes happen—"

"Oh my god, please stop!" My face is on fire! Mom and Keisha laugh, and I do too (after I scrub Mom's words from my brain). Mom and Keisha start talking about having a dinner party with Dani's parents, and I look out my window. Even though things went way off schedule today, it was kind of a good thing. I helped Dani, just like they've helped me so many times before. We talked, we laughed. And, just for a second, with Mom and Keisha embarrassing me, we almost felt like family.

Chapter 20

On the day of the runoff election, I feel nervous through all my classes, and as I walk to the clubroom, I feel sicker and sicker. Piper and Kyle believe Makayla's lie, but surely not everyone . . . ? There's no way they'd think I'm a mean person who bullies their sister. They know me. We've worked together side by side for a year and a half. They can't believe Piper's lie about me. I just have to trust them. I nod to convince myself, but I don't really feel convinced. I feel scared.

Dani meets me outside. They're grinning. "Ready to be president of the United States?"

"No, thanks. That sounds like an awful job."

Dani laughs and even though I'm nervous, I find myself smiling too. "We'll start with president of this club, then, yeah? Oh, that reminds me!" Dani digs in their backpack and pulls out a terribly drawn button. It reads, JANIE FOR PRESIDENT! and they've colored the background in red and purple, my favorite colors. "Surprise!"

I take the button, tears building in my eyes. I pin it carefully to my backpack, fighting the burn in my throat. "Thanks, Dani."

"No problem. Ready to go in?"

"I think so." I'm feeling hot, and sick, but also kind of hopeful. And I know Dani has my back. I worked really hard. I can do this.

Dani and I do our handshake, and then we enter the clubroom.

Everyone is sitting near the front of the room and Mrs. Clarity is here early for once. She motions for us to come up to the front.

"Come on! You're the last two voters!" She gives me a ripped-up piece of notebook paper and a pen. My head throbs in time with my heart; this is just like last time. But then, I thought for sure I had won. But it can't be like last time. They have to believe me, and not Piper's lie. But what if I didn't do enough? At least it can't be a tie again—all eleven of us are here today. My hands tremble as I write my own name on the paper, fold it, and give it to Mrs. Clarity. She smiles and collects Dani's too. Dani gives me a thumbs-up.

"Okay! Let me count the votes real quick . . ."

The room is silent while she tallies. Sweat beads on my brow and I try not to fidget. I glance at Piper and Kyle, but they're just staring straight ahead. Makayla tries to catch my eye, but I look away. Everything is so messed up—my friends, the schedule, Makayla. If I could just have this one thing. This one thing I wanted.

"Okay! All done!" Mrs. Clarity smiles at us. "It was very close. Everyone did such a good job."

I lean forward. Please. Come on—

"The new president of Sunshine Club is . . ."

I hold my breath. Please. *Please*.

"Makayla!"

I stare at Mrs. Clarity while the room erupts in cheers and clapping. This can't be real. This has to be a nightmare. This has to be a joke.

But it isn't. Dani looks at me, stricken, and Piper and Kyle hug Makayla, and the other club members crowd around her to congratulate her. Makayla meets my eyes, and she has the nerve to look shocked.

"Mrs. Clarity," I say, my voice weak. "I—I'm gonna step outside for a minute."

I don't know if she agrees. I stand and walk to the door, but it's like I'm not in my own body. My ears are ringing. My legs are Jell-O. I can't breathe. I can't believe it.

"You okay?" Dani's suddenly beside me, their hand on my arm. I can barely hear them.

I just don't understand. How did everything fall apart? I had everything under control. Mom and I had the schedule. We hung out on the weekends, and we got enough sleep, and Mom took her meds on time. Everything was fine. Everything was perfect.

"Janie?" Dani rubs my back, but I hardly feel it.

Everything was fine. My life was fine until Mom married Keisha. No, Keisha's okay, even if she's always late. The real problem is—

Makayla steps out of the clubroom, wringing her hands. "Janie? Are you okay?"

I stare at her and it's like something cracks inside my brain. Unfamiliar fire wells up inside my chest. "*No*, everything isn't okay!!"

Makayla flinches, but I don't care. For once I don't care what everyone around me is feeling. *I'm* feeling horrible, and I've held it in, and I can't anymore.

"What have I ever done to you, Makayla?! I really tried to be nice, and you stole my friends, and you lied to everyone, and then you stole my club!"

"Let's calm down for a second, Janie," Dani says, glancing from me to Makayla anxiously.

"No! I don't want to calm down!" Suddenly, I'm scream-ing. I've never screamed at anyone in my whole life. "She needs to know! This whole time I've been holding back, and I'm not anymore! You told everyone that I've been mean to you, but what about me?! You threw your freaking cat at me! I hate cats! I mean, I did get used to Pumpkin eventually, but you didn't know I would. I hate cats so much, and I never said anything because I was trying to be nice to you. And Mom and Keisha are always fawning over you, and I still didn't say anything because I wanted to be nice, and I knew it was hard to adjust to a new school. But then you blew me off to hang out with Piper and Kyle, who are *my* friends, and lie to them! They hate me now! They hate me because of you! They hate me so much they voted against me in the club we helped build together! And now you're president instead of me even though you just got here! Sunshine Club is my thing. This isn't fair. None of this is fair. This is all your fault!"

"Maybe you should go, Makayla." Dani's voice is soft and urgent, and really close. I blink and I realize they're holding me back, literally holding my arms so I don't rip Makayla apart. She backs away, but I'm not done.

"Don't ever talk to me again!" I scream at her. All that fire is pouring from my mouth, like lava out of a volcano. "I wish I never met you, and I wish my mom never married your mom, and you are *not* my sister!!"

Makayla is frozen, stunned like I've slapped her. I almost feel bad, but then I remember everything she's done and that fury burning in my chest swallows the regret whole.

Dani drags me away, down the hall and around the corner. As soon as Makayla's out of sight, I feel a lot better. I'm gasping, and my nose is burning, and I think I might be crying.

"Deep breaths, JV." Dani pats my back gently. "It's okay, we're okay. Deep breaths."

I try to calm down, but I can't. I still have that horrible crack in my brain. I still feel like setting something on fire. I still feel like I'm about to explode.

"Dani—Dani, I—" I still can't breathe right. "I . . . I . . ."

"It's all right. Come here." Dani pulls me into a hug, and

somehow their arms almost extinguish all the built-up fire in my chest. But now I have to face that I screamed horrible things at Makayla, things I can't take back. I can't figure out if I *want* to take them back though. I'm a mess. I lean against Dani and hold them tight. They're like a life raft.

"Let's go home, okay?" Dani whispers.

I can't go home. It's Thursday. I'm supposed to be at Sunshine Club until 5:30.

Except I never want to see the club I built from scratch ever again.

"Okay," I manage. I wipe my eyes with shaking hands. "But—but I think I need to be alone."

"Are you sure?" Dani frowns at me.

I nod. I'm sure. I'm a mixed-up puzzle someone dropped on the floor. I need to sort everything out, and then I can get back to normal.

"Okay. Can I stay with you until we get to your house?"

I nod again. Dani takes my hand and we walk home together.

It takes forever, almost forty-five minutes, but we don't say a word to each other. I can't. My brain is painfully blank. I just need an afternoon to calm down. It'll be okay.

We finally get to my house and I wave weakly to Dani. They wave back, worry all over their face.

"Text me if you need anything, okay?"

"Okay."

"And I'll be right over. Even if it's midnight. Not a second after that though!"

Normally I'd laugh, but I don't feel even close to laughing right now. "Okay."

Dani's frown deepens. "I'll see you tomorrow?"

It's a question, so I nod. Then I turn away and open my door so I can go to bed and cry myself to sleep.

Thankfully, no one is home, so I run upstairs to my room. Pumpkin is on my bed, but I don't care. I don't even care if she scratches me today. I climb into bed, disturbing her, but she doesn't bite or claw. She just meows in protest, and then snuggles under my arm. I hug her close and start crying, for the first time in three years, for the first time since we lost the apartment and everything fell apart.

Pumpkin purrs and I hold her, and eventually, I fall asleep. It's a relief to not have to think about anything at all.

Chapter 21

The next morning, I don't feel any better.

I'm so miserable. I'm so mixed up. I want to apologize to Makayla, but also I don't. I want to tell Piper and Kyle everything, but I'm so hurt they believed I could be mean to Makayla in the first place. And then I'm sad that I proved their doubt true. I *was* mean to her, in the end. And the worst part is that I think I meant what I said.

I don't know what to do.

I get dressed really slowly. Pumpkin watches me, occasionally putting a soft paw to my arm. I still can't believe she hasn't scratched me. I guess becoming friends with Pumpkin was one good thing about this new-family fiasco.

I wait until I hear Makayla go downstairs before going to the bathroom. I look in the mirror—I look terrible. My eyes are puffy and red from crying and lack of sleep. I wish I could just skip school, but I really need to try and stay on schedule. On what's left of it anyway. I brush my teeth and comb my hair, but it's like I'm moving in slow motion. I'm gonna be late. I can't muster the energy to care.

"Janie!" Mom yells from downstairs. "Hurry, baby!"

I sigh and leave the bathroom. Pumpkin meets me at the edge of my bed. She rubs her face on my arm.

"Wish me luck, okay?"

Pumpkin meows, and I pet her soft fur. I'm okay. I can do this.

As soon as I get downstairs, I know I can't do this. Mom, Keisha, and Makayla are all in the kitchen, eating breakfast. Keisha urges everyone to hurry while shoveling scrambled eggs into her mouth. Mom fixes Makayla's shirt. They all look so happy, when I'm the most miserable I've ever been in my life. I pause in the living room, watching my family exist without me. Instead of fire like yesterday, a wave of sadness hits me so strong I want to burst into tears. Again. I can't do this today. Not again.

"Mom," I call. Makayla looks at me immediately, wincing, but Mom doesn't look up from her plate. "I'm riding my bike to school today."

"What?" Keisha frowns at me. "We're leaving soon, Janie, I promise. We're late today, but—"

"No, that's not why." I take a shaky breath, refusing to look at Makayla. "I just want to be by myself."

"It's too far," Mom says. She's frowning at me too. "Go with Keisha and Makayla. They'll be ready soon."

"No."

Everyone is quiet, even me. Especially me! I didn't mean to say that . . . at least not out loud. I don't ever talk back to Mom. What is wrong with me?

Keisha comes out of the kitchen to the living room. "Is everything okay, Janie?"

I shrug, staring at her work boots. I think if I say anything, I'll cry again.

"Are you sure?" She puts a light hand on my shoulder. "You didn't come to dinner last night."

I nod, fighting tears. I hate that Keisha is so nice and Makayla is so awful. I feel really rotten about saying I wish she never married Mom. I don't mean that. I just wish Makayla hadn't come along too.

"Do you want your mom to take you to school instead?"

I think about it, but shake my head. I need more alone time, more time to get myself back to normal. "I just want to ride my bike, please."

Keisha looks back at Mom, then at me again. "Okay, you can. Let me know if you want to talk later, okay?"

"Okay." My voice is small. I wipe my face and turn away so I don't have to see her worried expression. At least Keisha cares. That's two people—her and Dani. And Pumpkin, if a cat counts.

I run outside and get on my bike. Maybe school will be

better. Maybe I'll feel okay when I get home. Though Saturday is Family Time, and I don't feel good about hanging out with my family right now at all.

Are we still on for Dani Time today?

I stare at Dani's text, feeling low. School was better—at least, all the classes I didn't have with Makayla were—but I'm so exhausted. I just want to sleep. Dani Time is on the schedule, like always, but I think today is another emergency. I think I need another Janie Time.

Not today

Okay. Dani adds several orange hearts. *Text me if you need me okay?*

I don't answer their text. Instead, I start the long bike ride home.

When I finally get there, winded and even more exhausted, Keisha's and Mom's cars are in the driveway. That's weird . . . usually Keisha's at work. I don't really think about it much. I park my bike in the garage and head inside.

Mom and Keisha are on the couch. Usually, they'd be cuddled up together under a blanket, but this time they're sitting straight, and they both look serious. It's like they're waiting on something.

"Hey, Janie," Mom says. She gives me a big smile. "You're home early. Not hanging out with Dani today?"

"Not today." My voice cracks a little.

Keisha glances at Mom, her expression anxious. "Are you feeling okay, Janie? Is there anything you want to talk about?"

I shake my head. I want to take a nap and cuddle with Pumpkin. And then maybe dinner . . . not that we'll be on time, but I want to try.

Mom looks at Keisha and they seem to communicate telepathically for a second.

"How about I go pick up something good to eat?" Keisha says, getting to her feet. "I'll pick up Makayla, and get dinner. It'll be a while, so you and Rosie have a lot of time to talk."

I nod, a little confused. It's only 4:00. Dinner is at 6:00. God, we're hopeless, even when Keisha has a rare day off.

Keisha pats my shoulder and leaves, glancing back at me and

Mom several times. I look at Mom after Keisha's gone, already tired.

"Can I go to my room?"

"Let's talk for a minute first." Mom leans forward slightly. "So, Makayla told us that you lost the election for Sunshine Club president."

New, fresh pain grates over the raw wound. "Yeah. I did."

Mom makes a sympathetic face. "I'm sorry, Janie. I know how much you wanted this."

Tears fill my eyes. I've been crying so much lately. It's like that crack in my brain broke something inside me. "Yeah, I really did."

"If it helps, this won't mean anything when you grow up. Just a little blip on the middle school radar."

That doesn't help. It's not a little blip now. "Can I please go to my room now? I . . . I don't want to talk about it."

"Not yet." Mom hesitates, then says, "I want to talk about this morning. Why didn't you want to ride to school with Keisha and Makayla?"

I shrug. I wish she'd just let it go. I'm so tired.

"Janie." Mom's voice carries a hint of warning. "Is it because Makayla won the election over you?"

I shrug again. My head hurts so bad.

"I know you're disappointed, but it's not right to take out your frustration on Makayla. We should always take the kind option, right?"

Some of the fire from yesterday sparks back to life. Why do I have to be kind? Makayla hasn't been kind to me in weeks! I grit my teeth and try to hold back the lava from exploding again. "I guess."

Mom touches my arm. "I know you're upset, and that's totally okay, but try to take it easy on Makayla. She's been through a lot."

The fire in my chest burns hotter. I can't hold it back. It's unbearable. Everything is unbearable right now. "Well, I've been through a lot too! Why is everything about Makayla?"

Mom looks stunned and I immediately feel guilty. I'm usually always calm, but this fire, this crack in my brain . . . I can't control it.

"I know you're upset, but this really isn't like you, Janie. What's going on? Really?"

I want to cry again. "Nothing. Can I please just go to my room, Mom? I don't want to talk right now."

"No, you're not going anywhere until you tell me what's going on."

I'm so frustrated I could scream. "Fine! I don't like Makayla. I don't want to talk to her anymore."

Mom's expression turns anxious. "Because of the election? Janie. I'm disappointed."

"No! I mean, it is because of the election, but also she put Pumpkin on my bed—"

"But she's always on your bed now."

"*I know*, but before, I was afraid of her! And Makayla stole my friends—"

"It's an adjustment, sharing your friends, but it'll smooth out soon."

She's not listening to me. She *never* listens to me. Hot tears sting my eyes. "Mom, please listen to me. Please."

"I am listening. I'm just saying that you can't be this upset over a club election, Janie. We're all family, you know? Makayla's your sister. And Makayla is my kid too."

I'm hot all over. And something inside me snaps, just like yesterday, and I'm on my feet in an instant.

"I'm not upset over the election! I'm upset because Makayla's a jerk, and you never listen to me!! I hate cats, and you let Makayla bring one here just because she wanted to! I live here too, Mom! I hated being scared to come home because there was a cat here! And I asked you to please let's follow the schedule like we used to, and you never do! You're always late picking me up now, and I hate it so much. I ask for one thing, just one, and you always ignore me!"

Mom just stares at me, apparently stunned into silence. I want to cry. I think I am crying. I want to hold back, but I'm so hurt, so angry, so sad, it comes out anyway.

"Makayla's your kid too? Fine. You can have her. You can have your perfect daughter and wife, and since Makayla has replaced me in everything else, you can just forget about me! I don't even want to be here anyway! I hate this family!!"

I don't wait for her to say anything. I finally stomp to my room, seething, sobbing. Pumpkin comes to me, meowing and rubbing against my ankles. I lean down to her level and hug her tight.

"Help me, Pumpkin," I sob. "It hurts. Everything hurts so bad. I don't know what to do."

Pumpkin purrs and licks away my tears. I hold her tight for a long time, but I don't feel much better. I'm so overwhelmed. I said it because I was angry, but it's true, isn't it? Mom and Keisha and Makayla are a family. They're happy, and I'm not. I'm just yelling at everyone and getting in the way. I feel so bad I wish the world would swallow me whole.

I'm about to cry again, but then I remember what Dani told me a while back, when Makayla first moved in with us.

If things get too bad, just run away, yeah?

My arms fall away from Pumpkin. I stare at all my dirty

clothes, my open backpack, the schedule on my desk. I dump all my homework out of my backpack, not really thinking about anything except for Dani's words. *Run away.*

I shove a few things into my backpack, including my planner, and open my window. "Bye, Pumpkin," I whisper. Pumpkin meows pitifully and it almost convinces me to stay. But I can't stay. I have to get out of here or I'll explode. I climb over the sill, climb down the tree in our front yard, grab my bike, and I'm gone.

Chapter 22

I've never run away from home before.

I feel kind of wild and dangerous. I also feel kind of silly. I ran off, but where on earth am I going to go?

I have my bike, so I just ride around town for a while. It's nice because I don't have to think about anything. But then I get tired, and hungry, and I look at my watch and it's already 6:03. I reach for my phone, but it's not in my pocket. Backpack maybe? I know I grabbed it . . . I think. I stop at the park so I can look.

I open my backpack and get even more depressed. I just grabbed a handful of dirty clothes and my phone and planner.

Not even a snack. I turn my phone on, and I don't have any new texts. No one's looking for me.

The urge to scream wells up in my chest and it pours out of my mouth before I can do anything. I just stand in the middle of Eagle Park and scream until my throat is sore. I want to break something, but I don't have anything to break, so I just throw my backpack down as hard as I can. I'm still upset, so I grab my schedule, my precious planner I've spent so many hours perfecting, and hold it in a tight grip.

I made this schedule for Mom. It wasn't for us, not at first. It was for Mom, so she wouldn't forget to take her medication, so we'd never lose our home again. I made it for her, and she doesn't even care. She won't even pick me up on time, or have dinner on time, or come to Family Time movies. She won't even listen to me when I talk. She won't even be on my side when Makayla has stolen everything from me. Even her. I open the planner, and with a savage tug, rip out a page.

After that first page, I can't stop. I rip them all out, in a frenzy. "I hate this schedule!" I scream at the sky. It was fine, but it's only been making me miserable lately. No, I've been unhappy for a while, and Lula and Dani and Keisha warned me, but I didn't listen. I just wanted to make sure Mom and I were safe. But since Mom doesn't care about me, I don't care if she has a schedule anymore either! Makayla can make her a new schedule and Keisha can remind her of her meds, and I can just disappear.

After I'm done ripping up the planner, I throw the outside binder in the garbage can. I look at all the fluttering pages in the wind, my whole life for three years, and the tears come again. Everything hurts so much. I really wish I could disappear.

I don't have any energy left after that. I ignore my buzzing phone in my pocket and pick up the pages and put them in the trash (littering is bad, even when the world is ending). I walk around Eagle Park for a while, but I think all the ducks were scared by my screaming, so it's not that fun. After a while, I ride my bike around town again. I don't notice it's getting dark until it is, too dark to see, and I look around. I'm next to the skatepark. I go in, and I'm the only person here. I think about Dani doing tricks on their board, how happy they looked. I toss my backpack to the side, and ride into the skatepark.

I don't know how to do any tricks on my bike. All I know is that speed is important, and all of a sudden I'm flying through the park. And for a second, it's fun. This is fun! The front wheel of my bike catches on the edge of a half-pipe and I go flying off the front. I land on my left arm and yelp in pain, but then I'm laughing. I was always so careful, so safe. And for what? I always just rode around, waiting for Dani Time to be over so I could move on to the next thing. I should have just learned how to do tricks with Dani. Why didn't I just have fun? Why didn't I do what I really wanted to do instead of following that stupid schedule?

I just lie on the ground, staring at the rocks and gravel. My arm stings, but I can barely feel it. Maybe whatever broke in me before I screamed at Makayla can never be repaired. Maybe New Janie is a yeller and mean and hurts Mom's feelings. Maybe New Janie wants to learn how to do cool tricks on her bike. I heave a sigh and close my eyes. I like one of those things. The others . . .

Footsteps approach and my eyes pop open. I'm staring at dusty tennis shoes instead of rocks.

"Janie?" Dani's anxious voice says above my head.

I look up at them and smile. "I fell off my bike."

Dani sighs, with relief or exasperation, I don't know. "And you don't even have a helmet on. Jesus." They hold their hand out to me and I take it. They pull me to my feet, and then put a hand on my back. "Let's sit down, okay?"

I nod, and they lead me to a bench. We just sit in silence for a while, but it's not bad silence. I'm glad they're here. I'm glad Dani, at least, doesn't want me to disappear.

"You know," Dani says after a minute, "when I said you could run away from home, I was kidding."

I laugh. It sounds exhausted, even to me. "It's all I could think of to do."

Dani nods, watching me closely. "Wanna talk about it?"

I shake my head, my eyes pooling with tears. "No. Please, not now."

"You got it." Dani is quiet again. I reach for their hand and they let me take it.

"I don't wanna go home. I can't. Not yet."

"You can come to my house."

"Really?"

"Yeah, of course! We can finally play *Resident Evil*."

I smile at Dani and they smile back. "Thanks, Dani. Also, I think my arm is broken." Dani gasps and I laugh, this time genuine. "I'm kidding! It is bleeding though."

"You need to remember your helmet and pads! Oh lord, you're giving me a heart attack!"

I laugh again as Dani fusses over my scrape. They grab my backpack and I walk my bike out of the skatepark, where Dani's mom is waiting in her car. She jumps out when she sees me.

"Janie! I'm so relieved. I have to call your mom right away—"

"No!" I wince at my desperate tone. "No, please. Please don't call her."

"I have to call her. She's really worried about you—"

"But Janie doesn't have to go home, right? She can stay with us tonight," Dani says, their expression hopeful.

Dani's mom looks from me to Dani, and then nods. "Okay. Climb in, Janie. What do you want for dinner?"

I wake up beside Dani, who's still sleeping. And snoring! I have to hold in a tired giggle.

It's Saturday morning, and I'm feeling better. A lot better than I did last night anyway. Dani and I had a late dinner, and their mom bandaged my scraped arm, and we stayed up really late playing *Resident Evil.* Well, we played the first ten minutes, then got too scared, then switched to *Cuphead* videos. Dani didn't ask me what happened, but around 2:00 a.m. I told them about my fight with Mom. And they just listened, which was a huge relief. They promised we'd talk about it in the morning, but now it's morning and I'm dreading it. I wish I could just stay here forever. But all the fire is gone, and what's left behind is guilt. I shouldn't have yelled at Mom. I didn't mean what I said about hating our family. I don't hate them. I just wish I belonged with them. I just wish they had followed my schedule better. Though since I ripped it up, there's nothing to follow anymore.

Dani wakes up and rubs their eyes. They blink at me and then grin sleepily. "Hey, JV. Did you sleep?"

"A little."

"Good! Hang on, I gotta pee."

Dani goes to the bathroom and brushes their teeth, and then after they're through, I do too. I have my own toothbrush here, even though I haven't spent the night in so long. Why not? Why haven't I done this in forever? No, I know. "Spend the night with Dani" was not on my schedule.

I come out of the bathroom and Dani is already back in bed. "Are you sleeping again?"

"Umm, yeah. It's, like, seven a.m. on Saturday! Come on, let's nap." They pat the space next to them and I snuggle in beside them. They cover me with their comforter. "We can sleep. Or we can talk if you want . . . ?"

I fidget a little. I didn't want to talk last night, but maybe I can now. "Umm . . . I just . . . I feel kind of lost."

"Yeah?"

"Yeah. Like I don't know myself anymore. Since when do I scream at people? At my mom? I love Mom so much and I screamed at her and said I hate her. And then I ripped up my schedule! What's happening to me?"

"Two options," Dani says, staring into my eyes. "One: You're turning into a werewolf."

We both giggle and I kick their bare legs under the covers. "If I am, I'll bite you so we can both be werewolves."

"Werewolf besties!" Dani's laughter dies and they're serious again. "Second option: JV rebranding."

"What do you mean?"

"I mean that the old JV was great, but something wasn't working. So you made a new JV. Still working out the bugs though."

I stay silent for a while, thinking about it. Maybe they're right. Maybe the old schedule worked when it was just me and Mom, but there was no way it could work with two more people.

So I need to make a new one? No . . . that's not right either. The old schedule didn't have bike tricks on it. Or spending the night with Dani. Or pop-up concerts, or *Cuphead* videos, or playing with Pumpkin. The old schedule didn't fix any of my family problems; it just made everything worse.

"We can think about it later." Dani yawns and closes their eyes. "At a decent hour. Like four or something."

I smile at them, and they smile sleepily back. At least I have Dani, and they don't mind Old Janie or New Janie.

Dani's door creaks open and we both jump. Dani's mom pokes her head into the room. "Janie? Are you awake?"

"No, we're both sleeping!" Dani complains.

I laugh a little before sitting up. "Yes, ma'am."

"Your mom called. She's coming to pick you up soon—"

"No!" I cover my mouth. New Janie is too wild. "I mean, no, thank you. I don't want to see her. Not yet."

Dani's mom frowns, but nods. "Okay, I'll tell her." She leaves and I lie back down.

Dani gives me an encouraging smile. "I like the rebranding. You stand up for yourself now."

"Yeah?"

"Just gotta tone down the screaming."

We laugh and I snuggle closer to them. They hug me and I nod off, warm and safe and feeling ten times better.

"Janie?"

I blink awake, groggy. Dani? No, not Dani . . .

"Shh, Mom! She's really asleep this time!" Dani hisses above my head.

"No, it's okay, I'm awake." I rub my eyes and sit up again.

"Sorry, but your stepmom called. She asked if it would be okay if she picked you up instead?"

I frown at my hands. I don't want to see Mom or Makayla. But Keisha has been really nice, and she's a good listener . . .

Dani nudges my knee. "If it gets too bad, you can come back. You can live here. We'll adopt you!"

I smile and then look at Dani's mom. "Okay. I'll go."

Dani's mom smiles. "Okay. She'll be here in a few minutes. And Dani's right; you're welcome here anytime."

Dani helps me pack my backpack, and gives me a big hug. "You're gonna be okay, JV. I promise."

I hug them back. "Thanks, Dani. And hey, listen . . ." I squeeze them tight and then step back so they can see my face. "You're the coolest person I know."

Dani grins and their mom calls me. I take a deep breath and leave the safety of Dani's room. It's scary, but I'm ready to change. I'm ready to see what New Janie can do.

Chapter 23

Keisha's face crumples in relief when she sees me. She looks kind of rough, which weirdly makes me feel better. I know I look rough too.

"Janie! Oh, honey—" She runs to me, and wraps me in a big hug. I hug her back, on the edge of tears again. I've been crying so much lately.

Keisha hugs me for a long time before pulling back. She searches my face, hers a little anxious. "I'm so glad you're safe." She gives me another quick hug. "Ready to go?"

I look back at Dani's mom. She smiles encouragingly. She

said I could come back if I wanted . . . but I think I'm okay now. I do feel a lot better. I look at Keisha and nod. "I'm ready."

"Okay." She pats my back gently. "I already grabbed your bike. Want to sit up front?"

I nod and she opens the passenger-side door for me. I get in and she does too, and I look back one more time at Dani's house. Dani's outside now too, waving frantically. I wave back as Keisha cranks up the car and drives away.

The closer we get to home, the worse I feel. I don't know if I can face Mom. I don't *want* to face Makayla. I sink down in my seat and wish I was back at Dani's.

"Have you eaten breakfast yet?"

I glance at Keisha. She doesn't seem mad at all. Just relieved. "Not yet."

"Wanna go to Waffle House?" Keisha smiles at me. "We can take as long as we want."

I breathe a sigh of relief. I don't have to see them yet. Thank goodness. "Okay."

Keisha drives us to Waffle House, and we walk in together.

She stays really close to me, like I'm going to run away again. She doesn't have to worry. I'm too tired to run anymore. My legs are so sore from riding my bike all afternoon and my arm still hurts. Running away from home is a lot more work than TV makes it look.

When we sit down in a booth, Keisha frowns at me. "What happened to your arm?"

I touch the bandage. "I fell off my bike. I was trying to do a trick, but I didn't really know how."

Keisha laughs. "I love it! But wear your helmet next time."

I nod, smiling a little too. I'm glad we're not talking about it. Keisha is the most patient person I know.

The waitress takes our order (I get chocolate chip waffles and Keisha gets eggs and hash browns), and Keisha tells me a story from her job. I'm listening, but I'm also kind of amazed— this is the first time I've ever been out with just Keisha. We made cookies together that one time, but we've never really gone anywhere together. I think I like it. It's nice.

"So," Keisha says. She's cutting her eggs carefully. "Are we ready to talk about what happened yesterday? No pressure."

I pick at a chocolate chip in my waffle. Keisha feels like a safe person. She won't judge me. "I think I just got really overwhelmed."

"Overwhelmed by the election results?"

"And . . . everything else." I can't bear to look at her. "Getting a new family is really hard."

"Yeah, I know. I agree." Keisha pats my arm, but I still can't look at her. "Tell me what the hardest part is."

There are so many hard parts. "I just wanted everyone to be on the schedule. Like me and Mom. But it doesn't work with four people. There's just not enough time."

Keisha nods slowly. I can tell she's really listening. "Do you want to try and make a new schedule? One that fits all four of us?"

"No . . ." I pause to think of what I realized at Dani's house. "I think it wasn't really helping anyway. I mean, it was, but it hurt us too."

Keisha is quiet for a second, so I look up at her. She seems thoughtful. "I think you're right. You made the schedule because you were worried about your mom, right? But she's doing better. You're doing better. You don't need it, Janie. You can live your life without worrying so much anymore."

I think about how fun it was at Dani's, and that the schedule never would have allowed that. I think about how Mom doesn't really need me to remind her of her meds anymore. She's late sometimes, and still gets really into painting, but she's always at the art gallery when she needs to be. I smile at Keisha, and a little bit of the crack in my brain seems to heal over. "I think you're right."

"Great! Problem solved. No more schedule." Keisha eats a bit of her eggs. "Now, let's talk about that argument with your mom."

Ugh, this is the hard part. "Do we have to?"

"No, but it might make you feel better."

I hesitate. Keisha's already helped me so much, so I guess . . . "I'm just mad at her because she never listens to me. Why didn't she know I don't like cats? It was so awful at first with Pumpkin. And I asked her to please follow the schedule, but she wouldn't . . ." I trail off, a wave of sadness engulfing me.

Keisha nods. "I know. We've really made a bunch of mistakes. Both of us. See, when I first met you, I thought you were the most responsible kid I'd ever met. And Rosie thinks that too. So, we thought you wouldn't struggle as much with the transition. But we were wrong. We didn't pay enough attention to how you were feeling. I'll let Rosie apologize to you herself, but I want to tell you I'm sorry, Janie."

I look down at my half-eaten waffles. I'm glad she apologized, but she didn't really do anything. Except be late for dinner, but that's not her fault. Apparently, fire station work is really hard. I want to hear an apology from Mom. And . . .

"I'm also very sorry about how Makayla has treated you."

I look up, surprised. How does she know what happened?

"Makayla told me everything. I'm disappointed in her and rest assured she's grounded for a while. But she asked me not to say much because she wants to explain herself." Keisha takes a shaky breath. "I know she hurt you, but I promise she wasn't trying to. She'll explain more, but I don't want you to think she hurt you on purpose."

"You're just saying that because she's your daughter." I wince. New Janie strikes again.

Keisha shakes her head. "No, I'm not. I mean it. And even if that were true, you're my daughter too. I love you both."

My eyes fill with surprised tears. This is what Mom said about Makayla. I didn't know Keisha felt like this too. Maybe I'm not kicked out of the family. Maybe I'm part of it after all.

We finish eating and Keisha hugs me again. "Ready to go home?"

I feel a little better. A little stronger. I nod.

Chapter 24

As soon as Keisha opens the door, Mom leaps to her feet. "Janie?"

I peek around Keisha meekly. "Hey, Mom."

Mom runs to me and gives me a big hug. I hug her back and she kisses my face like a hundred times. "Oh, Janie, don't you ever scare me like that again! What happened to your arm? Are you hurt? Where were you?"

I don't get a chance to answer Mom's rapid-fire questions. She pulls me into the house and puts me on the couch and starts fussing over covering me with a blanket. I laugh a little. "Stop, Mom! I'm okay."

"Okay, I'll stop. I'm sorry." Mom gives me one more hug and lets me go. She seems a lot more anxious than Keisha. She keeps messing with my hair. "Are you ready to talk? We don't have to."

I glance at Keisha, who smiles. "I'll leave you two alone for a while." She gives Mom a long look before going upstairs.

I look back at Mom and take a deep breath. "I'm ready."

Mom smooths my hair back again. "Janie, I'm sorry. I'm so sorry for everything. And we'll talk about running away later, but right now . . ." Mom takes a shaky breath. She doesn't look joking or easygoing at all. She looks serious for once. "I heard you, okay? I hear you. I'm not being a good mom to you right now. Things are so much better than they were before we moved, and I've been so happy, I can barely remember a time when we weren't. But you've been thinking about it, and I'm sorry I didn't recognize that."

Mom takes another breath. "If you want to get rid of Pumpkin, we can. If you want to reserve every Saturday for just you and me, we can. Whatever you need, Janie, tell me. I'm listening. I promise I'll listen from now on."

I fidget, a little happy, a little uncomfortable. I didn't expect her to apologize. "I don't want to get rid of Pumpkin. I like her, now. I just . . . I just wish you'd remembered that I don't like cats."

"I know. That's my fault, and I'm sorry."

"It's okay. Just maybe . . . let's not get another one."

Mom laughs. "Deal. And one more thing—I love you, Janie. I always will. Makayla isn't replacing you, okay? I was just giving her a little extra attention because she struggles with change, but I should have known you would have a hard time with this change too." Mom kisses my forehead and hugs me again. "You are my baby, and you always will be. I'm gonna do better for you. Promise."

I lean against Mom, all traces of my fury gone. Mom is gonna listen to me. And she loves me, and I'm not kicked out of the family. It's all going to be okay.

"Now, if you're up for it . . . Makayla's in her room. If you want to talk."

I don't really want to, but Keisha said she wanted to explain . . .

I tried being nice and that didn't work. I tried ignoring her, and that still didn't work. So, I guess I have to face her head-on.

"Okay. I'll try."

"You can do it. And listen, if you're still upset after you talk, that's okay. You don't have to forgive the people who hurt you."

"That's a pretty cool thing to say, Mom."

Mom laughs and pats my back. "I *am* cool! Now go ahead. After you're done, we can do anything you want today."

"Really?"

"Really. Saturday is Family Time, right?"

"Right. But . . ." I trail off. I'll tell Mom about my ripped-up schedule later. "And what happens tomorrow?"

Mom smiles. "Tomorrow you're grounded for running away from home."

I laugh. Finally, I'm not feeling so bad.

I climb the stairs, a little nervous. Pumpkin runs out of my room, yowling, and I stop to pet her. "Sorry for running away, Pumpkin. And hey, I saved your life down there. You were headed to the pound."

Pumpkin purrs and puts her paws on my shoulder, like she wants to be picked up.

"Sorry, not ready for that." But I do kiss the top of her head and smile against her fur. "Okay, I'm gonna talk to Makayla. Wish me luck."

I stand and go to Makayla's door. I'm nervous, but also ready to get it over with.

"Umm . . . Makayla?"

I hear the scrape of a chair and rapid footsteps, and then Makayla opens her door. She has dark circles under her eyes and she's still in her pajamas. "Janie! You're home!"

I nod. "Yeah. Keisha went and got me."

"I'm glad." She starts wringing her hands, but takes a deep breath. "Janie, I have to talk to you. I mean, you don't have to listen, but I want to explain."

I really doubt there's any explanation I'd accept, but I nod anyway.

"Okay. So first, umm, I'm really sorry about Pumpkin. I didn't know you were scared of cats; I thought you just needed to get used to them. You know, like exposure therapy? I thought if you got closer to her, you would see that she's a really nice cat and not like other ones."

Wow. I really don't like the idea of exposure therapy without my permission, but I guess I can see what she was trying to do . . . and, to be fair, it did work in the end. "Okay. But I am scared of cats. Not Pumpkin so much anymore, but other cats. I shouldn't have yelled at you, but I was really terrified."

"I know! I know. I'm not mad that you yelled. I just got really paranoid that you hated me after that, and you wouldn't want to hang out with me anymore."

"But I never said that . . ."

"I know, I'm so sorry, I just—I was overthinking. Because you said to forget it, right? And I thought you meant, like, forget being friends with me, because I'd done something unforgivable."

I just stare at Makayla for a few seconds. How could she think that? But I guess . . . I didn't really try to talk to her after that. I just assumed she'd be okay with talking on Saturday, when we were scheduled to. Oh. Oh man.

Makayla hurries to continue. "Anyway, when Piper asked me to go to the Glitter Bombs concert, I said yes because I thought you were still mad at me and wouldn't want to hang out."

This is starting to make a lot more sense. I should have reminded Makayla about the movie instead of assuming she still thought we were watching it together. No, I should have talked to her about Pumpkin a long time ago.

"Okay, I kind of get that. But then why did you lie to Piper and Kyle?"

Makayla hangs her head in shame. "I'm so sorry about that. I really didn't mean to. Piper asked me why you weren't at the concert, and I told her that we fought about Pumpkin and you probably didn't want to talk to me again. But then Piper took it way too far. She said she was so mad that you would do that, and someone who's mean to her sister shouldn't be president of a club about being kind and volunteering. And then she convinced everyone to vote for me instead. I didn't know it was even happening. And I don't even want to be president! I hate attention."

I shake my head slowly. Why . . . why would Piper do that?

I know we don't get along all the time, but she never even asked me what happened. I thought she was my friend. "Why didn't you tell her to stop?"

Makayla looks at the floor. "I never told you, but at my old school, I got bullied a lot."

"Really?"

"Yeah. It . . . it got really bad in the end. At first, they'd just leave mean comments on my Instagram, but after I deleted it, they started leaving notes in my locker. And then they started pushing me and stealing my books and backpack and stuff. I had to quit my old club because they would wait for me after school, when all the teachers were gone."

"Oh god, Makayla, I'm so sorry." Even though I'm still a little mad at her, I can't help but feel bad too. No wonder she was always exaggerating about school with Keisha. No wonder Mom and Keisha were always checking on her.

"It's okay. I mean, it's not, because it really made me scared. I was scared of not making new friends and being bullied again. So when Piper was telling everyone you were mean to me, I got so scared to tell her she was wrong. I thought she might try to hurt me." Makayla sniffs and looks up. Her eyes are full of tears, but also serious and determined. "But I was wrong. I should have been brave. Because I hurt you like those other kids hurt me. I feel so bad about that, and I'm gonna make it right, I swear. I'm gonna tell everyone that I lied, and step down from being president."

"Really . . . ?" I can't keep the cautious hope out of my voice.

"Really. I'm so sorry, Janie. You're a great sister, and I should be braver. Because we're family."

I turn over her words in my brain. She's right. We are family. And it's not like I was completely innocent; I didn't make time for Makayla because of my schedule and I never talked to her. I just ignored her, and when I thought she betrayed me, I was mean to her too. I wanted so badly for things to work out—the schedule, Mom, the election—that I ended up making every-thing worse. "I'm sorry too, Makayla. I shouldn't have yelled at you, and I should have talked to you instead of ignoring you all this time."

"So . . ." Makayla looks into my eyes, hers hopeful. "Are we cool?"

"We're cool. It's not a big deal—families fight sometimes." I smile at Makayla, and the last bit of that crack heals up. "And I forgive you. We can start over."

Makayla brightens. "Thank you, Janie. I really am so sorry. And for the record, I voted for you to be Sunshine Club president."

We smile at each other and I finally feel better. It was hard, and painful, but maybe worth it. I think, somehow, everything will be okay.

Chapter 25

At school on Monday, I stare down the hallway to Sunshine Club.

I had a nice weekend. I told Mom about my thrown-out schedule, and we agreed we'd keep some of it, namely getting to school on time. And also we agreed on Family Time, every other Saturday, when Makayla's home from her dad's. I texted Dani a lot, and we planned to have a sleepover this weekend, because Makayla won't be home. And maybe Tuesday, maybe some other day, Dani will teach me how to do tricks on my bike.

But now I have to face Sunshine Club. I'm nervous; I'm sure

everyone heard my meltdown. But I have to go in. No more running away. I take a deep breath and enter the room.

Dani is here already, so they make a beeline for me. We do our handshake and Dani smiles. "Happy to see you, JV!"

"Happy to be here."

Dani starts to say something, but Piper and Kyle approach us. Piper looks really uncomfortable and Kyle can barely look at me.

"Hey, Janie," Piper says.

So she wants to talk to me now? I almost say that out loud, but I've been trying to get New Janie under control. It's okay to stand up for myself, but not to be rude about it. "Hey, Piper."

"We're so sorry, Janie," Kyle blurts out. "Makayla told us she lied. Well, she didn't lie, but Piper kind of took it too far."

"Yeah, I did." Piper won't look at me. "I'm sorry. I guess I just felt protective, you know? Makayla told me what happened at her old school and I just wanted to make sure she wouldn't be bullied here."

"But why would you think I'd bully her? Why didn't you even ask me?"

Piper doesn't say anything.

I sigh. "It's okay. I talked it out with Makayla. We're cool now."

"Oh good!" Piper finally looks at me. "So see you at D&D? We added Makayla to the campaign so it'll be even more fun!"

"No, I'm good." I smile at her shocked expression. "I don't really like D&D. I just played because you and Kyle did. But if you both can't trust me, I think I should do something else with that time."

Piper and Kyle are speechless, so I nod at Dani and go to the front of the room to talk with Mrs. Clarity. She smiles when I approach.

"Janie! Makayla talked to me and she stepped down. She said she wanted you to be president instead. What do you think?"

I nod. "Yeah, I want to. But I want everyone to help with ideas, if that's okay?"

"Fine with me!" Mrs. Clarity says.

"But can I suggest one thing?"

She nods and I explain my plan. Mrs. Clarify smiles. "I think that's a great idea, Janie. Let's tell the others!"

At the nursing home, I meet Lula at our usual table.

"Janie, baby! How are you? Missed you last week."

"I know. I've been through some things."

"Wow, sounds like a very adult thing to say."

We laugh and then I reach into my backpack. "I have a surprise for you, Lula. Actually, two surprises!"

"Oh yeah?"

I give her a letter I wrote for Margaret. "I thought maybe we could try to reach out to your daughter again. I'm sorry I wasn't here for you when you needed me, Lula."

Lula takes the letter, a smug, triumphant smile on her face. "Finally decided to stop being so stubborn, huh?"

"Lula, come on!" I roll my eyes, but I'm smiling too. "I realized that the schedule was hurting me—yes, like you said. So now there's no more schedule."

Lula's smile softens. "I'm proud of you, Janie. I really mean that."

I round the table and give her a big hug. "Thank you, Lula. And I did something else hard—I made up with Makayla. We're cool now."

"Wow! Look at you!"

"Thanks. But now we have to do something hard too." I touch the letter in Lula's hands. "You'll send the letter, right? And talk to Margaret again?"

Lula sighs, but doesn't put down the letter. She holds it tighter instead. "Okay. But only if you're here with me."

"Deal."

"What's the second surprise?"

My grin gets bigger as Lula tucks the letter away. I pick up the cat carrier Mom dropped off before we got here and peer in at Pumpkin. She blinks at me and then starts purring, rattling the entire carrier. I turn her around so Lula can see her face. "Do you like cats?" I ask.

Lula gasps in delight. "Yes, I do! She looks just like my old cat, Mochi."

I set the carrier on Lula's lap and Lula lets Pumpkin out. The cat purrs and rubs her face against Lula's fingers. Mom said she can stay at the nursing home while we're at school sometimes; she absolutely loves attention, and now Lula won't be lonely when I'm not here. Somehow, everything really did work out.

For the rest of our hour, Pumpkin purrs in Lula's lap while we talk about cats and family, and how neither one ended up being so bad in the end.

Acknowledgments

The biggest thanks, as always, goes to Grandma. Though we fight over the smallest things, I know your love is everlasting, and I can never thank you enough for that. I still say the ideal room temperature is seventy-two!

Big thank you to my agent, Holly Root. You are an icon and a legend, and I'm so grateful for all that you do. Also, thanks to my fantastic editor, Olivia Valcarce. Thank you for being so kind and patient, and also for doing all my math for me! And innumerable thanks to Kieron for your expertise and patience! I'm so humbled and happy that you shared your experience with me, and I know Dani's character is ten times stronger because of it. Thanks also to the entire Scholastic team—you are all amazing and the work you've done on this book is immeasurable.

To my two best friends, Emily Chapman and Tas: Thank you so much for standing beside me when times got tough, and for all the memes and live tweets. And, fittingly, all the pictures of your lovely cats!

Special thank yous to J. Elle, Mary, and Gigi—y'all are my Big Three, and I always know I can come to you for advice, serious talks, and laughter.

Thank you to my writing groups: the slackers, WiM, Scream Town, and AltChat. You are all wonderful people and kept me going during this panini.

And, finally, thank you to younger Jessica—for staying. Cheers to many more books to come!

Find more reads
you will love . . .

Avery can sing, but hates singing in *front of people*. She likes to stay backstage at her new school, which is where, to her surprise, she finds a cat! As she sings to the stray one day, her crush, Nic, overhears her and ropes Avery into auditioning for the school's musical. When she lands the lead role, Avery knows she should be excited, but mostly she's terrified. Can Phantom the cat help her through her stage fright?

Have you read all the wish books?

- [ ] *Clementine for Christmas* by Daphne Benedis-Grab
- [ ] *Snow One Like You* by Natalie Blitt
- [ ] *Allie, First at Last* by Angela Cervantes
- [ ] *Gaby, Lost and Found* by Angela Cervantes
- [ ] *Lety Out Loud* by Angela Cervantes
- [ ] *Keep It Together, Keiko Carter* by Debbi Michiko Florence
- [ ] *Just Be Cool, Jenna Sakai* by Debbi Michiko Florence
- [ ] *Alpaca My Bags* by Jenny Goebel
- [ ] *Pigture Perfect* by Jenny Goebel
- [ ] *Sit, Stay, Love* by J. J. Howard
- [ ] *Pugs and Kisses* by J. J. Howard
- [ ] *Pugs in a Blanket* by J. J. Howard
- [ ] *The Love Pug* by J. J. Howard
- [ ] *Girls Just Wanna Have Pugs* by J. J. Howard
- [ ] *Best Friend Next Door* by Carolyn Mackler
- [ ] *11 Birthdays* by Wendy Mass
- [ ] *Finally* by Wendy Mass
- [ ] *13 Gifts* by Wendy Mass
- [ ] *The Last Present* by Wendy Mass
- [ ] *Graceful* by Wendy Mass
- [ ] *Twice Upon a Time: Beauty and the Beast, the Only One Who Didn't Run Away* by Wendy Mass
- [ ] *Twice Upon a Time: Rapunzel, the One with All the Hair* by Wendy Mass

Read the latest (wish) books!

a batch made in heaven

girls just wanna have pugs

J.J. Howard

alpaca my bags

Jenny Goebel

picture perfect

Jenny Goebel

Wish UPON A Stray

TAMIKE SAIED MENDEZ

meow or never

Anna Staniszewski

CLIQUE HERE

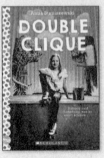

Anna Staniszewski

DOUBLE CLIQUE

Keep It Together, Keiko Carter

DEBBI MICHIKO FLORENCE

DEBBI MICHIKO FLORENCE

Just Be Cool, Jenna Sakai

TRUE TO YOUR SELFIE

MEGAN McCAFFERTY

pizza my heart

Rhiannon Richardson